THE WOMAN OF THE STONE SEA

BY THE SAME AUTHOR

This Place I Call Home (2010)
Zebra Crossing (2013)

The Woman of
the Stone Sea

Meg Vandermerwe

UMUZI

Published in 2019 by Umuzi, an imprint of Penguin Random House
South Africa (Pty) Ltd
Company Reg No 1953/000441/07
The Estuaries No 4, Oxbow Crescent, Century Avenue, Century City, 7441,
South Africa
PO Box 1144, Cape Town, 8000, South Africa
umuzi@penguinrandomhouse.co.za
www.penguinrandomhouse.co.za

First edition, first printing 2019
1 3 5 7 9 8 6 4 2

ISBN 978-1-4152-0938-7 (Print)
ISBN 978-1-4152-1040-6 (ePub)

Cover design by Gretchen van der Byl
Text design by Fahiema Hallam
Set in Adobe Caslon

Printed and bound by Novus Print, a Novus Holdings company

Ook in Afrikaans beskikbaar as *Die vrou van die klippesee*

For my father
For Graham
And for the men in the writing group at
Phillips State Prison, especially Carlito and Sly

Before this flood of thirst
and touch, before there was
flesh and longing and
blood, there was rain, there
was water, perfecting
everything that speech would
find and fill and lose again:

GRAHAM MORT

CHAPTER ONE

SUMMER IS AS GOOD A SEASON as any to commit suicide. That is what Hendrik has decided. So tonight he's standing up to his knees in the sea, ready to sink his siel beneath it. But fok, it's ice cold. Even a dronk man can't ignore it. He clutches the wine carton tighter. The sea is impatient. It's already filled his gumboots and is slowly inking up his broek. Wait, Hendrik thinks, let me first drink more. His brain is dizzy, ja. But Hendrik knows what wine can *really* do. Enough of it and the mind turns soft like baked apples. Then pain is distant. Heartache and hopelessness too. That's what Hendrik craves tonight more than ever.

Hendrik tips the last dregs from the wine box into his mouth and throws the carton into the tumbling water. He imagines it bobbing awkwardly, a clumsy boat. But the sea will never sink it; the foil inside will last forever. He himself has found all sorts of indestructible rubbish on these beaches, belched out by the waters. Once even a packet of orange pills with Chinese writing on them. He'd imagined the pills coming all the way from China, but most likely they were thrown overboard by 'n plat-ogies passing in one of the big cargo vessels, or poaching per-lemoen up the coast, on a night as dark as this one.

Tonight, even with the lighthouse's looping beam, the ocean is black. Hendrik closes his eyes and listens. The wine-numbness is starting. Goed. He focuses all his sens-es on the low roar of the waves, and on the breeze coming down from the koppies in the east. He can smell the salt of the ocean and the pepper of the fynbos. Like a mischie-vous child, the wind is slapping his ears, saying, Boo! Boo! And he can also hear the seespoke making their sukkel sighs. With every breaking wave, they exhale slowly like someone mourning the cards life has dealt them. Jaaaaaaa jaaaaaaaaaa jaaaaaaaaaaaaa. Sometimes there's a burp.

Time for another step. The sand sucks at his boots. He should have taken them off. Too late now. He wades deeper. In the daytime, seen from the fishing village above, the water is green and brown with kelp. It tastes bitter to a drowning fisherman, but sweet to the crayfish. Fresh kreef tastes of the sea, Hendrik thinks, but how does a man's flesh taste to them? He can feel Jakkals's eyes on him. He doesn't have to look back to know that the old bitch is shifting nervously on the water's edge. She's watching, baffled, as her master sinks deeper and deeper into the freezing black. Such cold always makes Hendrik's ball's tighten and now he wants to pis. He unclenches and enjoys the pleasant warmth as it seeps down the inside of his leg before washing away. Come on, another step.

The dog's running back and forth along the edge of the surf, white against the sand. She might bark, and you never know who's around. He should've locked her in the cottage. But when he tried, she began to scratch at the door and howl, as though she knew what he intended to do.

'Ag, we do not know why Jesus lets some things happen, Brother Hendrik. Mal things. But He knows. It is not for us to question ...'

Pastor Joseph's words after Rebekkah disappeared. Hendrik wanted to howl then too, a man made into a pathetic dog by shock. Now he just wants such memories permanently erased. Pastor Joseph meant well, and the others who offered sympathy with mugs of sweet rooibos tea, but their words were as useless as snapped fishing tackle. And why were they telling him they were sorry, and that he'd find a way to live without her, when she was coming back to him? What was the matter with them?

Although, after five years, even Hendrik sometimes has his doubts. The ocean can do it. If he lets it take him, it'll sink such gut-slicing doubts and memories so deep that not even Jesus Himself can conjure an opstaan.

Hendrik sways then wades forwards again. Jakkals is barking. Once, twice, three times. She's calling him back to shore.

'Shhht!' Hendrik hisses. 'Do you want to wake the whole fokken village! For fok sake. Shhht.'

The dog stops, but Hendrik can still hear her whimpering – far away now, behind a cotton-wool wall of wine. The water's up to his chest now. The seespoke are saying jaaaaaaaaaaaa jaaaaaaaaaaaaa jaaaaaaaaaaaa, over and over. No turning back. He sways and trembles as the waves and kelp fronds pound his body. The stones he gathered as Jakkals watched are making his pockets sag, stretching the wet fabric to bursting. They're there to drag him down. To make sure he does the job right. Hendrik grits his teeth.

'Rebekkah ...' he mutters. He's lost his train of thought. This water is boxing him about. All he knows is that their home has grown cold without her, as cold as this ocean. And the village ... He pushes his body deeper into the icy black. Ja, without her this is just a kak place. When he drives around he only sees rot and rubbish. The old white-painted fishermen's cottages with crumbling walls. The arrogant mansions built by inkommers, where there were once just dunes. The irritating seasonal tourists who clog up the roads in their BMW 4×4s with Cape Town licence plates, pushing up prices. And he's sick of being a crayfish man, of hocking his kreef to whoever will take them, and never for a fair price. Of the liquor store that won't give him credit, the snotty Richards girl on the till looking down her nose at him even though he's known her family since before she was a worm in her mother's womb. Of the tik addicts and the straatbraks whose bones jut out where their flesh is too thin. And the churches. Die pastore. The darkie pastors and Pastor Joseph. On Sunday mornings, hymns come through the windows of shacks as well as from the stone church. Those singing voices are high and hopeful. Driving past, Hendrik wants to slam his fist on his hooter.

And you know what, Hendrik thinks as he inches deeper deeper deeper, they stab the dogs, Rebekkah. The primary school children these days, they stab the braks, sommer for sport. He heard the Principal talking about it as they both queued to buy airtime at the one-stop shop. Meanwhile, across the country at this very moment, varsity learners are burning down campuses. Jissus, what a stinking mess.

But it's not our problem any more. Rebekkah?

He can't hear her. He can never hear her. She never replies. The seespoke sighs are growing so loud, they must be coming to get him. Boo! Boo! Boo! says the wind. The water is over his mouth and in his ears. Soon his feet will no longer touch the bottom. He can hear the strange booming of his own heart. The sagging stones in his pockets are calling him down. The aloneness in his bloed, in his brain, is calling him down. And the ghosts of all the sunken, the drowned, the lost. Saltwater is bitter to the drowning man. In the sunlight, if you hold it up in a plastic bottle, it's cloudy at first; then it settles and goes clear, with little flecks of seaweed in it. But at the bottom of the sea, the water is black and deep. Soon it will cover his nostrils and then he will let the seespoke and darkness finally take him, like a man.

What a fokken *nag*. Awful dreams. Hendrik groans as the memory of them slowly returns to him, like mental sooi-brand. He smacks his lips and pulls the blanket higher, sinking his bum deeper into the armchair. The inside of his mouth feels as dry as a piece of sun-bleached drift-wood. The droom … Urrrgh. It's coming back to him. Walking into the ocean, shouting her name. Hopeless. He meant to drown himself. But something had bumped up against his body. A blunt shadow, it carried him to the safety of the surface. What was it? A dolphin? He's heard stories of dolphins saving drowning fishermen and sailors. But this had hands and fingers. He felt an arm wrap around his waist. Pulling him up and up. Tearing the stones from his pockets.

A dom droom, you bastard Hotnot. But when Hendrik stretches, his big toe touches a sodden, sand-crusted bundle. He opens an eye and looks. Yesterday's clothes. So he did go into the ocean? And he really did try to kill himself? Fok.

He knows he's been feeling pretty depressed lately. It's difficult to keep up hope for his vrou's return when Rebekkah still stubbornly refuses to make any sort of contact. But he shouldn't drink so much dooswyn. What if he'd succeeded, and his Rebekkah came back today to find him dead!

But who saved him? And how did he get home? Ag, he can't explain it and hasn't the strength to puzzle it out. He's so tired and can feel a moer of a headache coming on. What he wants is for his Rebekkah to give him a hot cup of sweet, milky coffee to wash away this taste, like bokkoms in his mouth.

Hendrik dozes, then slips back into sleep. This time it's a real dream. As usual, it's of Rebekkah. She's wearing her yellow summer dress, standing in a schoolroom, waiting for him. When he walks in, he's so happy to see her. People have been saying you are dead, but I knew you weren't! I am so happy to see you, my liefde. He is crying. She smiles and shakes her head. Turns to the sink. Their sink and kitchen table in a schoolroom? But in the dream it all makes sense. She is preparing bread dough. Mixing the flour, salt, lukewarm water, a sachet of instant yeast in their pink plastic bowl.

But where have you been? Why did you not contact me? Do you know how hard it's been for me? She says nothing. The ingredients are mixed together. She turns the lump of dough out onto a wooden board. Her palms are working it. Kneading then pummelling, with her slender arms, her small fists. Tight-lipped. She will not tell him. She turns her pale green eyes away so that he's forced to look at the back of her head. Eyes the colour of the ancient jade that the divers once found off the coast here. Priceless, the newspaper said. From when the Portuguese sailed their boats past this tip of Africa, hundreds of years ago, their holds stuffed with stolen Oriental splendour – he can still hear Auntie K telling him and Anton all about it. Rebekkah? He calls her name in the dream. But she no longer seems to hear or see him. Instead she's laughing and talking with others. People he can't see.

Hendrik wakes. The sun is streaming in through the kitchen window. He is alone. The fridge buzzes softly. The house is empty. He gets up, staggers over the dog who yelps like he's really hurt her. She always does that, even if she just gets a skrik. He goes to the cupboard under the sink and takes out the last box of wine. Emergency ration. Twists off the lid. Swallows it down like water, in big thirsty gulps, then staggers to the bedroom clutching the carton to his chest and the blanket over his shoulders.

'Why are you not married?'

Rebekkah again. A few months after they met.

He climbs into the unmade bed. If he were to marry again, he'd marry Miss Klipdrift Brandy. Now that's a loyal woman. Never lets you down. Brandy is his favourite, but he can't afford it. He holds the wine box next to him in the bed, clutching it like the comfort lappie his mother gave him when he was six to chase away the night terrors and stop him wetting the bed. The plastic feels soothing against his face and bare chest. He takes another gulp, splashing red wine on the sheets. More wine is the only thing for beating off the babalas. It's better than a Panado or Grand-Pa Headache Powder. He closes the carton and turns. He can feel Anton's body against him. His exhausted older brother's teenage body, pressed against his in the bed they shared. Anton is snoring, his skin and hair stinking of sweat, brine and nylon crayfish nets. On his palms, Hendrik knows, are freshly burst blisters.

Hendrik wakes again gasping. The cottage is completely dark. He's slept through until nightfall. Outside the wind has picked up. It's rattling the roof and the windows in their frames and the sea is churning violently, like a seasick stomach, spewing its guts out against the shore. Something *was* in that water. Something or someone pulled him up. He rolls against the wall and almost crushes the half-empty wine box. Tomorrow he'll take the boat out and see what he can find. Maybe he's losing his mind; but he will go and see.

Hendrik is up before dawn. The last stars are in the sky and the moon is still casting her pale widow's glow. The other fishermen are up too, Hendrik knows, boiling water for their coffee flasks. Daryll with his 4×4 will be on the beach, ready to drag their small wooden fishing boats, their 'bakkies', over the sand to the water's edge. The official kreef season has begun and all the fishermen want to make the most of it, especially since the summer tourists have started to arrive in the village.

Hendrik pulls on a pair of pants and goes outside to the lewwetrie to pis, then finishes getting dressed in his yellow waterproofs and his gumboots. He shoves a slice of bread into his mouth and slips what's left of the wine into his rucksack. Something to keep the chill off his bones. He leaves his home chewing the bread. Jakkals trots behind. She'll watch on the beach as her master's bakkie boat passes out of view, then return to the cottage by herself, where she'll wait patiently in a patch of sun.

Once Daryll has dragged *Lekker* to the surf, Hendrik hops in with his rucksack and moves to the stern. The outboard motor spews its stench of diesel and the boat starts to bump over the waves. Concentrate, Hendrik thinks, as he swings the tiller west, heading out to sea. Jy moenie 'n ding misloop nie.

Hendrik picks up speed and heads south-east, back towards the deserted cove in the nature reserve where, two nights ago, he'd intended to take his life. The sun's coming up over the lighthouse, the ocean slowly turning from black to green. In the expensive guesthouses lining the beaches, yawning cooks are rubbing sleep from their eyes and chopping bananas and slicing paw-paw and cheese for the German tourists' breakfast buffets.

When Hendrik reaches the cove, he turns off the engine. He's close enough to row and there's enough light to see. If you're not careful, even with good visibility, the current can carry you along and, before you know it, trouble. A boat's wooden bones can smash as easily as 'n babatjie's. But he's been doing this his whole life. He takes the oars out from under the tarpaulin and drops them into the oarlocks. He positions the boat so that he's sculling at a right angle to the waves – harder that way for them to carry you onto the rocks. But Jissus, it's become tough work. His shoulders feel the strain as he rolls over the waves towards the shore. He's getting old, and not just in his body. The oars splash. Icy seawater sprays up, hitting his bearded cheeks and aching hands.

Finally, the water's shallow enough for him to jump out and drag the boat the last few metres onto the beach by its tow rope. The ocean, she wants his boat: she tries to pull it away from him, back towards open water, but he holds fast. He still hasn't seen anything.

It's only when the boat is safely beached, and he's buried the anchor into the sand for good measure, that he catches sight of her.

No, not his Rebekkah.

It's a black woman down at the water, her back turned. The cradle of rocks around her meant he couldn't have seen her from the sea. He's disappointed. Ja, he's not ashamed to admit it. Even after five years, it's the belief that she will come back to him that gets him out of bed each morning.

'Meisie! What are you doing out here?' A gathering wind scoops up his bitter shouts. 'Hey!'

She isn't moving. Is she ignoring him? Or maybe she doesn't speak Afrikaans. Another fokken darkie inkommer, Hendrik thinks, an outsider not born in the village. Last year, at election time, the ANC bussed hundreds of them in, all the way from the Eastern Cape. Darkies who couldn't speak a word of Afrikaans or even English. The government wanted them to sway the vote, but they failed. These days this village is loyal to the Democratic Alliance, a party that actually cares a fok for the Coloureds. Or so people say.

So what's she doing here in the reserve, Hendrik wonders as he walks towards her through the shivering fynbos. Gryp, that is all these darkies know how to do.

'Meisie! Girlie! What are you doing here? Private property. You can't squat or build your shack here.'

They bring crime too. Murder, robbery, verkragting.

It's completely light now. The water has that brilliant early-morning sparkle and he can see her clearly. With a grunt Hendrik pushes through another scrub bush. She's slumped over, body half in and half out of the water. If he were drunk, he'd think he was seeing things.

She's naked. Naked, but … Hendrik's eyes travel down. Lewende Vader. He stands gawping, his mouth opening and closing in silent shock, like a freshly snagged snoek's.

CHAPTER TWO

APRIL 27ᵀᴴ 2004. The day Rebekkah came into his life. People called it 'Freedom Day', because of Mandela's election ten years earlier. But Hendrik couldn't give a fok about 1994. He couldn't give a fok that for the first time in this country's history there'd been election posters with a darkie's smiling face on them.

'Do you see the almond shape of his eyes and his light complexion? Comrade Mandela has Boesman bloed,' Auntie K had crowed.

She was old by 1994. Old enough to have retired from teaching. Crooked with arthritis, Auntie K nonetheless remained active in the community, running a literacy group for adults and an after-school homework group for poor kids, who she fed with slices of brown brood topped with tinned pilchards in tomato sauce and glasses of sugary Oros.

'Boesman bloed se moer,' Hendrik muttered, when he heard Auntie K making her comments to Auntie Tilda outside the village's tiny petrol station. But he held his tongue and kept his peace as Auntie K went from fisherman's cottage to fisherman's cottage with flyers for Nelson Mandela and the ANC. She went to the whites' houses too, and to the house of old Pete who twenty years earlier had had himself reclassified from White to Coloured so that he could marry and live with the woman he loved. Her arthritic hips practically danced their way down the streets. Knock-knock, knock-knock. She banged on all the doors like she was the fish factory baas. Together she and Pete had waltzed and wept under a streetlight.

In her own cottage, she put the green, yellow and black ANC posters in every window. She even pasted one on the back of her old Toyota, the car that she gave to Hendrik before she died.

When the 27th came, that first stemdag, and it was time to join the long and patient queues at the polling stations, Hendrik stayed home and chopped wood. He did not cast a vote. He hasn't since. No Coloured right to vote or democratic government will ever justify the sacrifice Anton made to help make it come about. Nee. But Hendrik *does* care about April 27th 2004, because that was the day he saw her, his Rebekkah, for the very first time, at the annual Vryheidsdag Kerkbasaar.

Hendrik went not to support the church elders, but because Rolf, his sister Lattie's man, braaied the best Russians in the village. He stood by the smoking braai with

Rolf and Lattie and their eldest, Jarrad, home since December after finishing varsity, and waited with saliva gathering in his mouth for the first spitting sausages. All around people kuiered as the boombox banged out disco hits from the 1970s and 80s.

It was while he was standing there that he caught sight of Rebekkah across the crowd. She was wearing a cardigan and her white dress. She was the new primary-school teacher, come to teach the Grade Is, Rolf said as he flipped a red sausage with his braai tongs. But what everyone was talking about was how she behaved with the street dogs.

'It's a church, a holy place on a holy day, not a kennel. These inkommers have no respect for how we do things,' Lattie complained, serving Hendrik a white roll and Russian with a squeeze of sticky chilli sauce.

For the past three Sundays, since her arrival in the village, it seemed Rebekkah had been feeding the braks after church. Now the dogs gathered in packs, waiting for her.

With a mouth full of sausage and tangy sauce, Hendrik asked, 'Where's your Christian charity? Wasn't Christ kind to animals?' He took another slurp from his can of Coke and wiped chilli sauce from his beard.

'Ja, Ma, she's not so bad. Maybe you should try talking to her.' His handsome and usually confident nephew looked awkward as he spoke up for the inkommer girl with the long black hair.

Ten months later, when he and Rebekkah were courting, Hendrik would long to run his fingers through that soft, straight hair.

'Hou op, Jarrad,' said his ma. 'As for you—'

The way Lattie looked at Hendrik, he knew what she was thinking. Who are *you* to talk of charity and the holy book? As far as she was concerned, her brother was in partnership with Lucifer – ever since he told her that, after what happened to Anton, he didn't believe in church or Jesus.

Hendrik ignored his sister. Swallowing another mouthful of Russian, he turned away. He wanted more information about this woman, this pretty inkommer who'd got everyone hot under the collar.

'Did you know her at varsity?' Hendrik asked Jarrad when Lattie had gone to get change from the women selling fluorescent crucifixes.

'Ja, sort of—'

Before they could talk more, Jarrad's fiancée, Michel, appeared. She was the daughter of Pinkie Booyens, the crayfish factory manager, a rich man who had shares in the factory and also sold smoked snoek on the side. His daughter had Jarrad wrapped around her spoilt finger. She didn't even acknowledge Hendrik as she took Jarrad's hand.

'Daddy wants to address the flock, but the microphone won't work.'

Hendrik thought he saw Rebekkah watching them as Michel led Jarrad away.

On the Sunday that followed the basaar, Hendrik decided to go back to the kerk to see Rebekkah. He arrived for twelve, when he knew Pastor Joseph would have long since stopped his gesnap and everyone would be socialising over cups of tea, slices of melktert and a good skinner. Hendrik looked out of place in his takkies, jeans and t-shirt among all the people in their bright, pressed Sunday best, clothes they kept aside for church, weddings, funerals and school graduations. Immediately he scanned the crowd for Rebekkah's face. He'd brought her something.

She was across the road by the bushes that overlook the beach. She was standing alone, staring at the water. In her hands she held a plastic bag. Kos for the braks, he thought. Hendrik approached her, avoiding Lattie, whose eyes he could feel drilling into his back.

'For the dogs.' He gave Rebekkah the small newspaper parcel. Bones, left over from a beef stew. All week he'd been keeping them for her, and when she thanked him, he tried not to smile from pleasure.

'They're a bit dry. I kept them in the fridge.'

'They won't mind.'

Hendrik watched Rebekkah approach the braks waiting on a little scrap of concrete behind the church. This was where she always fed them, and they wagged their tails when they saw her and her plastic ice-cream containers filled with rice and chopped-up white bread and other leftovers.

But when they saw him, they dropped low and were reluctant to come forward. Hendrik knew that look. Hulle is bang. His, Anton's and Lattie's faces used to show the

same when their Pa came home from Pete's boat workshop stinking of liquor, with anger on his breath.

As well as the dogs, Rebekkah made people talk because
of the flowers. She wanted to plant and grow flowers, she
told him one afternoon maybe ten or twelve days later,
when she stopped him unexpectedly in the one-stop shop
and asked him to drive her to the Agrimark. He nearly
dropped the Gatsby roll he was eating.

'Why do none of the other Coloureds in the village
grow flowers?' she asked him.

His hands were shaking, so he gripped the steering
wheel tighter until his knuckles turned almost white.

'So you're Jarrad's uncle?'

'Mmmm.' He could only grunt when Rebekkah asked
him questions about himself.

'I met him at varsity, did he tell you?'

'Mmmmm.'

'You catch kreef too?'

'Ja, mmm.'

He could feel the sweat pouring down his neck and
armpits and soaking the back of his T-shirt. Did she notice?

In the large shop, popular with local farmers, she didn't
let him push the trolley as they went from aisle to aisle collecting what she thought she needed. Plant food, manure,
seeds and potting soil. She would hang flower baskets too.

'Where are you from?' Hendrik blurted out as last, as
she bent and lifted a ten kilo bag of manure onto the trolley. It smelt like musty meat.

She shrugged, 'Die Karoo.'

He'd heard of that. 'Don't your parents worry about you staying so far from them?'

'I never knew my parents,' Rebekkah replied.

A white man standing next to them in shorts, with a very pink face, loaded bags of bone meal onto his trolley with a stifled grunt. Hendrik waited for him to push past before asking his next question.

'So who raised you?'

'My ouma and oupa. My mother's parents.'

She spoke well. He enjoyed listening to her. Her Afrikaans was polished, like a fresh stick of teacher's chalk. She spoke a bit like wit mense, like Auntie K could when she so chose. Like the educated. It was because she studied to be a teacher, he told himself, just like Auntie K and Anton. They make teachers speak like that, even if when they go home they slip back into their own taal. Hendrik had not even sat his matric, was just a fisherman who'd never finished a book, although he still read the newspaper most days, like Anton had taught him. But Rebekkah didn't act like she considered herself too good to spend time with someone like him.

'Tell me a story, about your people.' That's what she asked him when they got back to her tiny rented cottage with the manure and trays of pansies.

'I haven't got many happy stories for you,' he warned, pushing the spade into the ground. He'd insisted on doing the digging, wouldn't take no for an answer.

'Jirra, a man has his pride!' he told her, taking the spade from her and thrusting it into the earth.

She shrugged and let him do it.

As he was digging, he couldn't help himself. His brain was churning faster than an outboard motor. You and I, we can make happy stories together. Then one day, when our children ask …

They hardly knew each other and she must've been twenty years younger than him, his nephew's age, but in his heart he knew, already then he knew, one day he would maak haar syne.

Suddenly Rebekkah put a hand on his shoulder. It was the first time she'd touched him, and he froze.

'Tell me about your parents,' she said with a smile.

He shook his head. 'Nee.'

'All right, tell me about you, when you were a boy.'

This is Hendrik's first memory. He's on the beach with a blue bucket. He is with Anton. Anton is carrying the knife, even though they don't need it. Their mother's sent them to look for witmossels. Normally they go with her, but now she's too busy with the new baby, who seems to spend her time only howling and shitting. The sun is as bright as a blade and the warm air smells of summer and salt. Today, Anton's doing something different. Instead of dancing the twist on the tideline, drilling with his feet to find the mossels sommer by luck as Mama has taught them, Anton goes down on his knees and begins to sniff the sand.

'They smell like pampoen,' says Anton.

Hendrik goes down too, but he can only smell salt as the

sea foam sloshes around his ankles and knees, wetting his shorts and palms. Suddenly, he's frightened. What if someone sees and tells Daddy? Will Dêrra think they're up to mischief when they should be working? Anton is still on all fours, sniffing the sand like a dog following a scent.

'Ek wil nie meer speel nie!' Hendrik cries, leaping up.

'Is okay, I think I've found some. Help me dig.'

Hendrik falls back onto his knees and begins to dig like his brother has told him. It's nice to dig in the wet sand. The tin plates they're both using scrape back the sand without much effort, like pushing a spoon into warm porridge.

Hendrik cannot believe it. The mossels are there, pale as fingernail moons, just like Anton said. It was like magic. Like Oom Daniel when he mos pulls a fifty cents from behind your ear on your birthday.

'Daarsy!' Anton dropped them with a clank into the bucket.

For the next hour they moved down the beach, Hendrik keeping watch as Anton sniffed on all fours. Soon the bucket was so full that only Anton could carry it.

Afterwards they played in the rock pools. Anton told Hendrik stories about all the creatures that lived there. Starfish, he said, they once lived in the sky like the other stars, but one day it rained so hard they fell into the ocean and grew their funny suckers.

Hendrik laughed. But Anton didn't laugh. He kept a straight face, then shrugged, 'You don't have to believe my stories, but they're all true.'

Suddenly Hendrik wasn't sure if his brother was lying
or not. After all, hadn't he said he could smell white mussels through the sand because they smelt like pumpkin,
and he actually could?

'Tell me another.'

'You see those birds with the rooi ...'

Seals had once been people, Anton said, and mussels
were whale spit washed up and hardened to the rocks.
After the stories, there was even time to swim.

Before they entered the house, Anton put his hand on
Hendrik's shoulder.

Hendrik could see the droplets of seawater still in his
brother's hair.

'Don't tell Dêrra or Mommy how I can smell mossels.
Moenie iemand vertel nie.'

CHAPTER THREE

JA, SHE'S STILL ALIVE. He wasn't sure as he carried her over the cottage threshold like a moonlit bride, wrapped in a piece of tarpaulin. Now that she's in the bath, the tarpaulin tossed aside and Jakkals krapping at it, he can see clearly that her chest is rising and falling, although she still won't open her eyes.

They have hearts, he thinks. And tieties, just like Rebekkah said, like a normal woman, despite the great fish's tail. Lekker, firm ones too.

When he first found her by the rocks, she was unconscious, completely stiff, and he thought that if she wasn't dead already, she would be pretty quickly if he didn't do something. He splashed her with seawater and wrapped her in the tarpaulin, then hid her in his boat and ran to fetch the Toyota. The whole way back to the cottage, his heart was banging in his head. Waiting for Rebekkah to come back has finally made you mal, he told himself. His rubber boots slipped in the sand. He tried to keep to hard, wet stretches.

When he got home, he grabbed the Toyota keys from the table and drove straight back to keep an eye on the water maiden. At nightfall, he knew he could bring her back to his cottage safely in the darkness, with the neighbours asleep and only a few cars on the road. He loaded the still limp creature into the back of his car, more tarpaulin under her to save the upholstery.

He knows this creature is linked to Rebekkah somehow. She had stories about such creatures. He remembers her lying next to him in the dark, speaking dreamily: 'When I was a girl on the farm, Ouma told me stories. About water maidens. When I was a little ... even as a teenager, that's what I wanted to be. Beautiful and free in the water like them.'

He turned on his side then and put his palm on her stomach. One day it would swell from his seed. He imagined what it would be like to feel their son's heart beating through her stomach's flesh, under the scar on his wrist where he'd caught it in the net once. My bloed. My bloed groei in haar.

'A mooi silver tail and long blonde hair. Completely free,' Rebekkah repeated with a yawn. 'I looked for them all over the farm, in all the dams, but never saw one.'

'Blonde?'

'Ja, Ouma said so.'

'And light brown skin?'

He felt Rebekkah shrug, 'In some lights it sparkles.'

'Oumense se gelofies!' he snorted.

Hendrik felt Rebekkah stiffen beside him. When she spoke again, her voice was frostbite. 'My ouma didn't tell lies.'

She turned her back to him and Hendrik found himself shut out. He rolled over. Fok. She fell into her moods so suddenly, especially when it was her time of the month – rooikappie. Lattie was just the same, although not Mama. Their hormones went deurmekaar and the man was left like a drifting boat without a fokken anchor.

Okay, so maybe your ouma *didn't* tell lies, Hendrik thinks, looking down at the creature now in his bath. But this one isn't light brown with gold hair, Rebekkah. Her stert *is* silver like you said, sure, but she is a darkie. As swart as looking out onto the ocean on a moonless night, and her hair is short and curly on her head, like a normal darkie woman. Not one who has all those artificial things woven into it to make it look like the hair of wit mense. Hendrik remembers his own mother sleeping with a kous on her head every night to make her kroes hair straight.

And she's hurt. Standing over the visvrou, he examines her wounds without touching her. There are cuts and gashes on her arms, hands, back and one on her right cheek. Her great stert, more than half her body, looks unharmed. What did it? Not a shark. She would be crayfish food if it was. No, the wounds are too minor. Nothing down to the bone. Rocks? The cuts are too thin, too regular. Nee. They look like they've been made by barbed wire. The little bit of congealed blood that lines them is dark red. So tieties, a heart and red blood, just like a normal person. But a great silver fishtail, strong and sturdy like a giant tuna. He felt that spine bone as he carried her. Her fin is yellow and black like a tuna's too, only it has bits of brown, like a kabeljou. To be honest, in all his years of fishing he's never seen a fish with a tail quite like hers.

He's not sure what he expected. Rebekkah never spoke about their fins, or their hearts or if they bled. He wishes she was here. She'd know what to do with this watervrou. Or if not Rebekkah, her ouma. That old woman seemed to know about such things. He'll have to keep an eye on the wounds and make sure she doesn't start to go slimy. A bad sign for a fish. He needs to wash his T-shirt, which has spots of her blood on it.

Once, when he was a boy, Hendrik saved a male vink that had been chased from its nest in the tree next to their house by the female. In fear, it spun into the windowpane and made Hendrik jump. You could tell it was male, because it had a yellow beak and was more beautiful than the female ones, which don't need colours to court. He was sitting at the table after school, eating a slice of bread smeared with peanut butter. For some reason, he can't remember what, he was the only one home. Stunned, the little weaver, small as a kelp gull's egg, lay completely still on the ground; he had no trouble scooping it up. He held it in his cupped hands for a long time, more than half an hour. All the time he thought, please don't let Daddy come, nie nou nie. Dêrra would make him throw it out, he was sure. The little vink's breast pumped so hard, Hendrik thought it would die of a heart attack. He'd heard that animals can do that, die of skrik. But not humans.

Although, he thinks, there was one woman in the village whose hair went white overnight. Not from fear but from grief. Haar baba dood in die bed. No one knew why, just stopped breathing. She found it cold and stiff the next morning, its tiny lips tinged blue as a bruise. For years after that, Hendrik saw her walking in the street, her hand holding tightly onto the arm of her remaining little blonde-haired boy. She died long ago. The sugar took her, but people say really the diabetes was caused by the heartbreak of seeing her little girl in the coffin.

Hendrik stands up and catches sight of his reflection in the bathroom mirror. He doesn't like to look at his own face any more. He was once aantreklik, like Anton and Jarrad. But since Rebekkah went, his hair and beard have been going grey and his skin looks sallow, like a piece of brown bread that's turned mouldy or like an old, dead fish that's lost its shine and is starting to stink. Hendrik stares down at the breathing visvrou.

'Wat dink jy, Jakkals? Do you see her too?'

The dog looks at him and rolls on the tarpaulin that Hendrik dumped next to the bath.

'If I'm not careful, they will have me by the hospital with the mal mense.'

Still, if she *is* real, she'll want water, he imagines. Not tap water. Seawater that smells and tastes like her ocean home.

He picks up the galvanised buckets next to the fire-place and tips out the coal with a clank. Immediately Jak-kals sniffs and scratches at it. He'll need more containers than this, if he is to fill that bath before dawn. What else? He opens the cupboard. A basin for washing up. Another plastic bucket with a broken handle and a dead daddy-long-legs in it. He tips out the spider's curled corpse. They will all need to be taken to the beach and filled, then brought back as soon as possible, although she doesn't seem to be suffering out of water. Not like a real vis. Cray-fish can last, even in the freezer, although they go into a coma. But not fish … They suffocate in our air, Hendrik thinks to himself, imagining a flapping, gasping snoek. Drown in our oxygen, same as we as humans drown in their oceans.

Friday late afternoon. The visvrou has been in his home for almost twenty-four hours. All night and most of the day, Hendrik stayed in and watched her. He was waiting for her to disappear, to prove she was just in his mind. But she didn't. Each time he went into the bathroom, she was still there, die heeltyd eyes closed, body limp in the water, tail half in and half out of the bath. If it wasn't for the soft hiss of her breathing, he'd have thought she was dead. But no. Her scales still shone nice and bright. And she didn't have that sliminess that a fish gets when it's going vrot, or the stink.

By 3 o'clock he was vrek moeg, but he had to go out, or risk not getting paid this week. He had kreef deliveries for his handful of private clients, and for the factory – Jarrad's very strict about when stock is delivered, even with him. Ever since his nephew married into the Booyenses and took on the job as accounts manager at the factory, he seems to have forgotten who his real vlees en bloed is.

Now Hendrik has finished his last delivery, to a retired Coloured couple who come each summer from Cape Town to spend two months in their holiday home in the village. The man was born here, but he's done well for himself, with a booming construction business. They always give Hendrik a good price.

A pair of darkie women walk past the car, towards the location at the edge of the village. Hendrik watches them. Probably nakkas, he thinks, but from which African country he can't make out. All night long the settlement will thump and throb with music and chatter because today is pay day and everyone wants to dance, laugh and drink their troubles away before Monday comes and it must all start over. Those that aren't getting drunk are in one of their informal churches, throwing up their hopes and prayers like mooring ropes to God.

Maybe she'll be gone when he gets home. Or maybe she'll be dead.

Hendrik rolls down the window. The streets are full of white tourists and their cars with Cape Town and Gauteng licence plates. He drives past the crossroads near the entrance to the village and sees the burnt-out shell of

Auntie K's old house. The other morning, he saw someone had sprayed RONEL in red paint inside one of the
rooms. He wonders who RONEL is. That same house is
where his Auntie K fed the schoolkids pilchards, brood
and her political rubbish. Now it's derelict. After her
death there was a fire. No one knew who set it. There'd
been fighting about who would claim it, because she had
no husband and no children and had made no will. Now
the tik users go to it every night. It makes Hendrik think
of a haunted house. Anyway, it's not my problem, Hendrik thinks. He's delivered his kreef on time, so at least he
has money in his pocket and can go and quickly buy some
supplies and another carton of sagte rooi.

When Hendrik gets home with his wine and shop-
ping, he goes straight to check on the visvrou. Turning on
the bathroom light, he finds she has slid down in the water so that her head is submerged. Her tail is now flopped
over the end of the bath and Hendrik must shuffle past
carefully so as not to brush against it. Those fin tips look
dangerously sharp. Her eyes are still closed, but Hendrik
can tell from the mess of water on the linoleum that something has gone on. Maybe she rolled over for pleasure, the
way seals do, turning their silky, glistening bodies in the
water. So she's definitely still alive. And her wounds?
Hendrik peers down. They don't look worse. Ja-nee, they
might even be looking better. Saltwater must be doing
them some good.

Hendrik goes back into the kitchen and unpacks the
groceries and wine box. He needs a drink. Just one though.

He must not sink under tonight. He needs his wits about him in order to figure out what to do. All day while he was watching her, trying to figure out whether she was real or just some figment that he'd conjured from too much box wine, he considered contacting television stations and maybe also newspapers. He's seen the *Daily Star* headlines at the one-stop shop: 'Tokoloshe ate my wife', kak like that. Maybe he could make some money out of her.

But then came worries. What if she *is* just in is head? They'll send some reporter with a photographer. Hendrik will lead them into his house to meet his darkie mermaid and … nothing. Just a bath filled with slimy seawater and floating kelp. Mrs Simons, Lattie, Jarrad, all the members of Pastor Joseph's flock would hear about it and want their faces in the papers too. Before he knew what hit him, it would be *his* life that was the nuus. 'He used to be such a good man. Until. You know his brother … He was murdered in the struggle, and then his wife … she … Now he drinks. Forty-five but doesn't he look seventy? Ag shame.' And, 'If only he took Jesus into his heart.' That would be Lattie, or Jarrad's wife, Michel. Michel is as dull as watery soup but at least she knows how to give his nephew children. They have three kids under ten and another on the way, judging by Michel's swollen maag when Hendrik saw her skinnering with Lattie in the street last week.

Hendrik would rather drink boiling chip oil than swallow anyone's pity, he thinks as he unpacks the dog food and the lamb chop he's bought himself. And if she *is* real, well, then there's the strong possibility that maybe Rebekkah has sent her with a message. Didn't she always say she wanted to be a water maiden? Wasn't she the one who first told him about them? Ja-nee. Until he can figure what is what, he's sitting tight and not doing anything rash.

Jakkals is looking up at him expectantly, waiting for the rattle of dog biscuits to fill her bowl. Is the visvrou hungry too? What does her sort eat? Rebekkah, what do I feed her? Rebekkah always knew how to tend to sick animals. Only this visvrou isn't exactly an animal, she is human too. A half-vis, half-human darkie. Hendrik twists open the wine box, pours himself a large glass and gulps it down. Fok.

He puts Jakkals's food down. Soon the dog will go out and make a drol that will sommer steam in the night air. Another gulp of wine. He'll build a fire. Then he'll try and feed this half-vrou, half-vis darkie. If she eats it, well then, she can't be in his head.

Wet wood hisses in the grate when you light it. Kak, man. Tyrone promised him the lot was dry. Hendrik squats and lights another match and tucks another ball of crushed newspaper under the pile. His body is already warmer from the gulps of sagte rooi, but he gets cold at night, even in summer, so sometimes he makes a fire. He knows how to build a good one. That was one thing his father taught him.

'Moenie die hout so styf pak nie. That's reg. The flames need space to breathe, like a man.'

Hendrik and the others tried to make themselves invisible whenever their father came home late, stinking of sweat, engine grease and beer. Anton, Lattie and Hendrik would gather in one corner of the cottage, where the bathroom now is. Their mother, too, would talk to them in whispers, even before their father came home, her thin frame tense.

He should have stayed on the ships, he'd say when he was in a particularly bad mood. 'Then I wouldn't have to make myself sick with the sight of all of you.'

But the whole family knew that their father had only lasted three months when he went to work on the huge cargo ships down in the Cape, when he was sixteen.

It wasn't all foul weather with their father. Sometimes the bastard could be all right. He'd make them laugh by serving their mother her tea from a tray and showing them how it sommer worked when you were a steward for the officers on the ships. He would fold a lappie over his sleeve. Ja, their Dêrra had a lekker sense of humour when he wanted. But it all seemed like a funny game to him, keeping them on egg shells, never knowing what to expect. He'd saunter in, his face like a brewing thunderstorm. Hendrik would brace himself for the worst. Then, without a word, Pa would empty his pockets. Toffees and half-cent Chappies bubblegums would roll out, and packets of cheesy NikNaks for Hendrik and his siblings to scramble for. That's what Hendrik hated most about him. The bastard was unpredictable. One day he might give you five cents for sweets. Another day, make you laugh so you wet your pants as he imitated how the moffie stewards minced as they served at Captain's Table. But then when you least expected it, when you were just passing his chair as he spooned mince into his face, slap the back of your head so hard that you bit your own tongue and the taste of blood filled your mouth, salt and iron. No tears, though. Tears were weakness. A sign of wanting pity and therefore an excuse for a lekker bliksem.

Hendrik gets up from his haunches and goes to the table. He cuts a slice of bread before putting the loaf back in its plastic bag in the breadbin. What else? Kaas, Rebbekah? He cuts a thin slice of hard yellow cheese and puts it on a plate with the bread. Why a plate, he doesn't know. He doesn't imagine that such creatures use plates. There are no plates in the sea, although maybe they use shells like in that cartoon his niece used to watch when he and Lattie still talked and visited each other. Hendrik shakes his head. Stop being dom, man. He goes to the bathroom and switches on the light. Ja, still there. Still floating in the water like a dream.

He offers the visvrou the plate. The gashes on her cheek, forehead and shoulders look much better. She seems to heal fast. He drops some pieces of cheese and bread into the bath and waits. The cheese sinks. The bread floats. No, she's not interested. She keeps her eyes closed. What do they eat, darkies like her? Pap en vleis? Isn't that what they like?

He doesn't eat much meat at the moment. Too expensive. But he's hungry, and tonight he'll treat himself.

Lamb is his favourite. It used to be beef, but Rebekkah taught him to have a taste for tender lamb. He goes back into the kitchen, unwraps a chop and takes the frying pan out of the cupboard. Rebekkah reorganised this kitchen when she moved in. These past five years, he's tried to keep it just the same, so that when she does come home to him, she'll find it as she remembers it, and know that all along he thought of her.

Hendrik pours a glop of sunflower oil into the pan, gives it thirty seconds to get hot, then drops the chop in with a hiss. He cuts another thick slice of bread to sop up the juices. In the fridge there's half an onion and some sliced tomato. He'll put those on the bread too, with margarine and the pan juices and the meat.

The meat sizzles as he waits for it to turn brown. He likes it well cooked. Jakkals is looking up at him — she's smelt the chop and knows she always gets the bone. Hendrik flips it with a fork. The whole house now smells of sweet frying lamb fat, making his mouth water. His mind wanders to the visvrou's silver-brown fish scales. When he picked her up out of the water and wrapped her in the tarpaulin, they were softer than he expected. But at the same time, flexible and tough like fish scales tend to be. Before you can cook a fish you must scrape the scales off with a vlekmes. They fly everywhere, dotting your face and clothes like tiny, bloody petals. He taught Rebekkah how to do it, but she never enjoyed it and one day she simply dropped the knife and the fish and refused to vlek again.

Hendrik turns off the gas and lifts the chop onto his plate. With his knife he cuts off a piece of lamb for the water woman. Jakkals's black eyes follow him as he puts it on a separate plate.

He stands in the bathroom entrance, a precious slice of meat waiting for this water woman if she'll just open her eyes and show some interest.

'You eat meat?'

No reaction. He doesn't usually have an appetite for darkie women, but he supposes this creature is beautiful, just like Rebekkah said they were. Not just her face and top half, which are like the face and body of an attractive African woman, maybe like a pop singer or someone famous on television. Her fish half, too, has a nice shine to it. If he ever caught such a lekker blink vis, he'd consider himself lucky. In the electric light her scales twinkle like Christmas tinsel.

He looks at the meat, then again at her. 'Why have you come, visvrou?'

It was his birthday. She'd brought homebaked rusks and a flask of steaming coffee and two tin mugs. The rusks were a little dry, but he ate three in a row from nerves, letting the crumbs spills into his lap and onto the blanket they were sitting on, as all around them families unpacked picnics and put up sun umbrellas and children squealed with delight in the surf.

It has taken weeks to get her here. After he helped her to dig her flowerbeds, she hardly replied to his texts and made every excuse not to see him. He was confused. Was she very busy at school? Two weeks after their trip to the Agrimark, he drove past her cottage and saw all the flowers were already wilting. Soon they would be dead. He wrote to her again, offering to take her back to the shop. Silence. Maybe she's angry, he thought. Should he have warned her that her flowers wouldn't grow? That the flowers she chose would never make it in the salty sea air and the sandy soil, even with the help of the manure? Wild fynbos was the only thing that grows in the soil of this village. But his tongue had been all twisted like rope.

He waited another day then smsed:

'Do you like 2 swim?'

Silence. Still nothing. Finally, Hendrik asked his sister to send him a text: 'I think there's a problem with my phone. I'm not getting sms.'

In reply Lattie sent, 'jesus is my verlosser.'

Trust her to send him a fokken test sms like that, Hendrik thought, before pressing delete.

Four more days passed with nothing. It was almost a month since he was last in her company. He could feel his heart losing hope. After all, why would a woman like Rebekkah be interested in a man like him? But he couldn't help himself. Hope floats, like seagull kak. He took to waiting outside the school when the learners were leaving in the hopes that he'd bump into her. In his mind he rehearsed what he'd say: 'I thought we could go for a coffee, or a walk?' But he never managed to catch her.

By the following Sunday, his longing to be near her

was so strong that he decided to go back to church. When he arrived, the service was not yet over, but he saw Rebbekah standing outside talking with Jarrad. Hendrik felt a shiver, like pins and needles, travel down from his brain, to his throat, to his stomach. They were standing very close, she and Jarrad, but when they saw him they moved apart.

'Good morning, Hendrik,' Rebekkah said. To his surprise, she hugged him. 'Jarrad was just telling me about one of my pupils. A little girl whose mother works by the factory. There are problems at home. Very sad.'

'I need to go back inside,' his nephew said. Nodding at Hendrik, Jarrad left the two of them alone.

'I've been trying to reach you. Have you not been getting my SMSes?'

'Ja-nee, sorry. School's been keeping me very busy.'

'Can I take you out?'

She was silent for a moment. 'Look Hendrik, I must tell you, I'm not looking for a boyfriend, okay, only a friend.'

Hendrik felt like he'd been slapped, but he wouldn't give up so easily. 'Fine,' he lied. 'Next Saturday is my birthday, can we go out then?'

On the Saturday at 10 a.m., he collected her from her cottage. After the rusks on the beach, he took her to visit the lighthouse. It wasn't dark, so he couldn't show her how the lighthouse's beam illuminated the fog so it looked like the breath of a spirit. He'd wanted to show Rebekkah that. But he could at least take her inside.

Earlier that week, he'd climbed to the top and stood in the lantern room, looking out to sea and then down onto the red dirt road that led to the reserve. I'll bring her here, he'd promised himself. Bring her here and teach her all about this lighthouse. He wanted to show her that he was not a complete doos. Even though he hadn't been to university like her, there were things he did know. Like about the village lighthouse and other local history. She'd been to study, so he imagined such things interested her. And afterwards, in the coming weeks, months and years, he told himself, he'd take her to all his secret hiding places from when he was a boy. The beach where Anton first showed him that he really could smell witmossels. To the place where he and his brother found a beached whale. When it died, its enormous tongue stuck out, white and bloated. The whole village came to look. It made him feel nervous to look at the dead whale. Its tongue hung out obscenely, like a man caught with his pants down and his piel out. It made Hendrik think something bad was going to happen. Still, it was interesting and he wanted her to know about it.

As Hendrik and Rebekkah stood in the lantern room, he explained to her about the vuurtoring's special flashing heartbeat. This one flashed every fifteen seconds, he told her. Every lighthouse beam flashes in a unique sequence, so that a lost seaman or fisherman would know which point along the coast he'd reached when it was night and they couldn't see land. Then he recounted those dramatic few days with the whale. How everyone came to try and save it, the fire brigade, sea rescue, some wildlife fanatic.

'One old Auntie, Auntie Matilda, she was mal, man. She claimed she could talk to animals. She was always talking to something. Dogs, cats, birds, even ants. She claimed the other whales told her it had done it on purpose. That it wanted to die.'

'Maybe she could talk to them,' Rebekkah replied. 'You don't know that she couldn't.'

Her expression was flat. No smile. Was she messing with him? Maak sy 'n grap? It was the sort of thing Anton would say.

'Why did you come to live in our village?' he asked her.

'I wanted to be by the ocean.'

'There must be oceans closer to where you're from?'

'I always wanted to stay by the Atlantic. We learnt about it in school. Across that ocean was America and Michael Jackson. We all loved Michael Jackson at my school.'

'He is also mal. He's made himself look like a white and like a woman.' Hendrik said this even though when he was a young man, he worshipped Michael Jackson as much as everyone else. But he'd become a blerrie moffie. Hendrik thought about telling Rebekkah about his father's imitations of the moffie stewards, but when he turns to her, she's frowning.

'I want to go home now.' She drew her purse to her and, without a word, began to climb back down the ladder.

When they reached her house after a silent drive in which she did not speak, she accused him of having mocked her.

'I wasn't mocking you, man. I was just saying—'

But it was no use. She was already out of the car, walking to her door without even a goodbye. Watching her go, Hendrik felt something in him break. A feeling a little like panic came over him. He was thirteen again, watching Anton walk with his suitcase to the bus stop and the bus that would take his brother out of his life and to the foreign land of the Coloured varsity near Cape Town.

CHAPTER FOUR

SEVENTY-TWO HOURS since the visvrou's arrival, and Hendrik is now certain that she's not looking hundred per cent. Earlier, when he checked on her before climbing into bed, he could see in the single hanging bulb's light that her scales were not shining as brightly as they had been; he's worried that they'll soon grow sticky with mucus, a sure sign that she's on the way out. He can hear his mother's words, 'A sick fish soon goes vrot.'

Lying on his back in the dark, Hendrik peers at the ceiling that is Cremora white in the moonlight. One of the neighbour's television is blaring skiet en donner and the dog is rubbing her head against the side of the bed. Jakkals is always scratching. She has wax, black and smelly as tar, in those shaggy white ears. But if he tries to clean them out with a lump of toilet paper, she mos snaps a piece off him, so she must just make her own plan. Her rubbing is keeping him awake, though. If it continues, he'll put her out.

The water woman didn't touch the meat, and for some reason he couldn't bring himself to eat her portion. He gave it to the dog, Jakkals so white and curly that with a good dose of wine in him it made him think, lam eet lam. Although Jakkals is no lamb.

'Careful. She looks like a skaap but she bites like a jackal,' Rebekkah always warned the village children. 'When you need to catch an orphan lamb on the farm to feed it with the bottle, you pull it like this, by its one back leg.' Rebekkah, laughing, bent down and tugged hard at Hendrik's right ankle, so he lost his balance. He fell forwards and knocked his head with a thud against the Toyota's raised bonnet – he'd been checking the radiator because the car was giving trouble, but the mechanic was closed for the holidays. His tumble only made Rebekkah laugh harder. Then, suddenly, she stopped and her eyes went cold.

'Fok, Hendrik, sometimes you are so dom!'

Hendrik turns on the light. The memory of Rebekkah's laughter fades and he tunes his hearing to the sleeping house. Another sound. A radio? Neighbour's television? No, something else. Shrill and plaintive. A high-pitched moan ... It throbs in Hendrik's head like a dull toothache.

He leans back into the pillow and listens hard. The sound, and with it the throbbing, is getting worse. With a terrible jab of pain, he realises it is the water woman. She is suffering. He grits his teeth. He can't bear it. He *must* find her something to eat.

Hendrik gets up and pulls on his jeans and jersey.

'Come on, Jakkals.'

The dog looks at him, confused.

'Nee, not another midnight swim. We've got to find our darkie something to eat before she goes vrot on us. Kom!'

The dog stands up and stretches, then yawns, showing a pink curl of tongue.

The holiday houses on the road leading down to the beach are all still lit up. The tourists and visitors from out of town have arrived, smearing everything with their noise and money. Hendrik prefers it when these houses are dark. When they're a part of his quiet, self-imposed exile from other people.

The moon is high and bright and the sea ghosts are sighing as loud as ever. Hendrik walks quickly down to the rocks with his flashlight, pocket knife and a bucket. The tide is low enough for the rock pools to be exposed. He'll bring back all he can find. Some mussels, some seaweed.

Hendrik remembers when he and Anton were boys, if the catch had been poor or their father had drunk away his catch money and their mother's crayfish factory wages, she'd take them to the rock pools to look for veldkos. The pools around here used to be teeming with life. You could go for a walk and stop at any rock pool and discover all sorts: starfish, skaamkrappe, small shoals of tiny, darting fish. Almal weggewyk. Even in the reserve. Some say it's pollution or global warming, or the big trawlers that scoop everything from the waters like a greedy child gobbling up all the chips at a party. Others blame the fishermen themselves. There are still mossels though. The village Coloureds still go and harvest them for bait or for the pot, even though you're now supposed to buy a licence from the post office for the privilege.

'Nee, sies! A licence for food that is free and doesn't belong to anyone but God Himself.' Lattie was angry when talk of the new, more expensive foraging licences first started.

Another memory. No stopping them without a drink, especially in this place, near the stretch of shore where Rebekkah was last seen. Daryll says he greeted her, but she didn't reply. She was standing, stokstil, up to her ankles in the surf, looking out to the silver horizon.

Daryll knew about Rebekkah's moods from Hendrik. He himself was walking off too many Black Labels from the night before at the Red Sail. He'd had a row with his vroutjie and their new baby had been colicky all night, so he'd taken himself off to get some fresh air before heading off to meet the fishermen further down the beach. Neither Daryll nor anyone else actually saw Rebekkah enter the water. But everyone knew she liked to swim by herself, even early in the morning, and since women don't just evaporate and since no one saw her leave the village by the small dirt road, it was decided that she must have paddled out and been swept away by a sudden strong current.

'But are you certain it was her?' Hendrik asked his friend over and over until Daryll, unable to take it any more, put his hand on Hendrik's shoulder and said, 'Hendrik, it was her all right. It was your Rebekkah. Boet, you have to accept that the ocean has taken her.'

But Hendrik knew that Daryll was mistaken. Rebekkah might have been on the beach early that morning while he was getting *Lekker* ready. She might even have been in one of her moods, which meant she didn't greet his friend. But she didn't walk into the water. Somehow, and he's not exactly sure how, she slipped from the village.

Ever since that summer day five years ago, he's wondered where she is. Did she go to the city? Did she move to another seaside village? Has she gone overseas as staff on a cruise ship? Maybe she's even back home, in the Karoo dorp of her birth. Although when he went there to look for her, two weeks after her disappearance and then again for her ouma's funeral, there was no trace. He was chasing hope like a dog chasing the wind.

To keep going on the long drive, he used a trick a cousin once taught him. That cousin drove lorries delivering fish from the factory all around the country. He showed him how you make a potent cocktail of a can of Coke and six tablepoons of instant coffee. The caffeine in that could keep a man driving for a day and a night, although the body gets the shakes and the mouth develops a strange, bitter taste. Hendrik tried not to stop, but he needed to get petrol and once he needed to pis. As he shook off his piel, he stood for a few minutes just looking at the electricity pylons, the lines and lines that ran across the orange-brown landscape like sewing thread. A single silver windpomp, with a clump of green under it, turning slowly, bringing water silently up to the surface from far beneath this dry earth. So this was the landscape his Rebekkah came from. This was her stony land. He could understand why she longed so much to have the blue blanket of ocean fill her vision. Here the only blue was the cloudless sky.

'Rebekkah never told us she was married. My husband would've liked to have known before he died.' That was what Rebekkah's ouma told him when he finally found her on the farm the following morning. She was a small woman, small as a young girl, but with a wrinkled, shrunken brown face. She showed him to the only proper chair in the two-room labourer's cottage. She didn't seem surprised to see him, although she had no idea who he was.

Hendrik didn't know what to say to that. For a moment he thought he might cry, so he asked for a glass of water. The old woman said she would make him some rooibos tea instead. As she was boiling the water on the gas burner, she asked him about himself and the place where he'd met Rebekkah. 'There used to be a sea in these parts too,' the old woman told him, 'long, long ago.'

Hendrik thought about the dusty stone valleys and rock koppies like giant knobbly knees that he'd passed for hours and hours. But he nodded politely and quickly swallowed the rooibos in his cup.

Finally, he felt strong enough to ask his questions. Did

she have any idea where her granddaughter might be? Had she ever done anything like this before? To both questions the answer was nee. Never. Hendrik felt despair but he refused to give up. He thanked Rebekkah's ouma and gave her his cell number and made her promise to phone him if she heard anything.

As she was walking him back to his car, the old woman asked again where Rebekkah was last seen.

'On the beach.'

'Maybe the water maidens took her.' Did Hendrik want her to perform the rituals needed to get her back? She would be home before school started the following week, her confident grandmother said.

No, he told her. She is just away. His response was automatic. A repeat of the story which he'd been telling himself over and over.

The drive back was not easy. The whole way, terrible questions tormented him. Why had Rebekkah not told them about her marriage? Was she ashamed?

When he got back to the village, he went straight to his sister's place to collect the dog. But Lattie took one look at him – 'Lewende Vader!' – and put him to bed.

He wishes now that he'd asked the old woman to do those rituals of hers. But at the time he had no patience for silly old woman's fantasies.

The soet rooi is in the house. Should he turn back? No, he needs something for the moaning creature to eat. So the memories come as relentlessly as the tide as he steps in the darkness from illuminated rock pool to rock pool, dropping whatever he can find into his bucket, his torch-light guiding the way.

When Hendrik gets back to the cottage, he finds the visvrou has submerged her face under the water again. Relieved that the moaning has stopped, he peers down at her. Ja, the wounds are almost gone, but her scales definitely look duller. He tips everything he's found into the bath with a splash, and waits. She makes no effort to acknowledge his offerings with good grace. She doesn't even open her eyes.

'Eet!' he commands, angry. 'Or do you want to die? Is that what you were doing on the rocks?'

It never occurred to him before. He thinks of Auntie Matilda's story about the whale that beached itself. Hendrik looks down at the unmoving visvrou.

'Do you know my Rebekkah? Did you water people take her?'

CHAPTER FIVE

FIRST LIGHT. Hendrik is heading out over the waves in *Lekker* to visit his offshore crayfish traps. The other fishermen are on the beach. Rolf, Oskar, Daniel and Pieter, all wearing their bright yellow rubber waterproofs and gumboots. Soon Daryll's 4×4 will pull their bakkie boats across the sand and out into the surf. Others are already on the water. All the kreef fishermen are keen to make some quick and easy sales to the crayfish-hungry tourists. By selling to them direct, they're able to get round the factory quotas. The other men all greet Hendrik, even though he no longer drinks with them or shares a smoke. Since Rebekkah's disappearance, Hendrik is a man who keeps to himself.

To get the good kreefs, the big, juicy ones, each man has his special spot. You can't put your traps in another man's spot. It's like sticking your piel in another man's wife. And you inherit your spot: Hendrik's was his father's, and his grandfather's before that. It should have been Anton's, but by the time his brother was old enough, he no longer believed in the life of the visserman. Ja, he was going to save this country instead, by becoming a teacher and stirring up the kids with words and self-belief and politieke praatjies.

You should have stuck to kreef and stayed away from the darkies and the politics, brother. You might still be alive, Hendrik thinks as he pulls up a cage and prays for a catch. Inside there are three, no four, fat, long crayfish, and only two kleintjies that are too young and must be tossed back. A good day. There are already seven others in the cooler box. He lifts its lid and, holding them by their antennae, drops the fresh ones in. Then he re-baits the trap with mackerel heads and lowers it again. Some men use limpets or mossels as bait, but Hendrik only uses oily fish, makrielkoppe or geblikte sardientjies just like his daddy did, and his ma's pa before him.

When he gets home, he goes straight to the bathroom with his ice chest. Even before he opens the lids, she stirs. When she smells the crayfish, she opens her eyes – green like the ocean. She starts to swish her tail excitedly. Water from the bath sloshes over the side and onto the linoleum.

He takes out his pocket knife and sticks the blade into the centre of the first kreef's head, killing it. He holds it out to her and a wet hand grabs it. Snap. She twists off the head. Her teeth are white like pearls. Her hands are surprisingly dainty, though her fingers are long and strong as she crams the meat hungrily into her mouth. Pink tongue, Hendrik thinks. Soos ons.

Rebekkah is chopping onions at the table. He sees her. Her slim figure in her pink dress, stooped over her work. The rhythmic tap of her knife slicing through onto the wooden chopping board. Then the lamb: sticky stewing meat, chopped into squares. Her fingertips roll the pieces in flour before dropping them into the pot to sizzle and spit in the vegetable oil.

He looks again at the visvrou. It doesn't seem right to watch her eat. He leaves the rest of the crayfish in the open ice chest next to the bath. At least four hundred rands worth, although he hasn't had time to weigh them. Jakkals sniffs at the kreef as they wriggle and struggle to climb out, but the cooler box is too deep.

'Kom, Jakkals.'

As he leaves the room, the dog at his heels, he can hear the water woman's tail sloshing the bathwater excitedly. He lets the dog out; Jakkals will scratch when she's done her business and wants to be let back in.

Hendrik sinks into the armchair and puts his head in his hands. They stink of bait. He is suddenly vrek moeg. But at least he now knows for certain that she's real. Only a real thing could eat a kreef. He'll have to go out again tomorrow and hope the kreef have taken the bait. If she's going to eat his crayfish, he'll have to catch extra to feed her and have enough for the factory. Another crunch from the bathroom. Another one gone. He wonders how many she can eat, will need to eat, in a day, a week. Ten? Twenty? Thirty? She could bankrupt him.

It doesn't seem that her sort need to kak or pis either. He can see no sign of it, although the water has turned a deeper green – but that could be the seaweed and kelp fronds he's added to it. Still, he doesn't look too closely when he goes in there. Even though she's not completely human, it doesn't feel right. Like watching a cat scrape a hole to do its thing. Cats are funny like that. Full of pride. A dog doesn't care. Jakkals will leave her business anywhere she likes the smell of. But a kat, she has her dignity and will bury what she does. Will give you the stink-eye if you try and watch. He remembers Auntie K's cat. It was run over and when Anton helped her find it, he told Hendrik he found it with its eyes popping out of their sockets.

'The Egyptians worshipped cats. Their Pharaohs were black like us.'

One of Auntie K's history lessons.

'Pa says we aren't black. The kaffirs—'

He stops mid-sentence, in shock. She's slapped him, and his cheek burns from the blow.

'Never again in your life let me hear you using that word! You understand?' Auntie K's voice shimmered with rage.

Hendrik nodded. He was too afraid to speak. His palm pressed against his stinging cheek.

'Your dêrra is fokken dom. To the boere, it makes no difference. We are all "nie-blankes", non-Europeans, so just different shades of "kaffir", verstaan jy?'

Snap. Another one. Hendrik imagines the water woman sucking out the raw, firm flesh. When there's been a period of silence, he goes back to the bathroom. The cooler box is empty except for the shells. She's excavated the bodies and delicately crunched her way through the heads, antennae and all, and dropped the empty river-mud coloured shells into the chest. Once again she's slipped her head beneath the water. But Hendrik can see that now she is smiling, her eerie green eyes still open and fixed on him like stars.

CHAPTER SIX

THERE SEEMS NO SATISFYING THIS VISVROU'S appetite for kreef. She's just gobbled down seven, and is now splashing in the bath, which is her way, Hendrik knows by now, of demanding more. She must've eaten twenty, at least, since he discovered she's lus for them yesterday. He's tried to give her snoek or pilchards, he even tried mackerel-head bait, but no, it's only the crayfish she wants. Sjoe, these water maidens have expensive tastes, Hendrik thinks, as he goes to the icebox to fetch three more. He doesn't want to calculate the rands he could've made selling these beauties to the tourists or even to the factory, rather than watching them disappear down her greedy, dark gullet.

Hendrik sits at the kitchen table and picks up his pocket knife and his kreef trap. This trap's an old one that needs mending. He cuts through the rotten nylon and takes out his spool of thread. He'll bind the place where the hole is so that nothing can escape. As he cuts, he can hear the visvrou playing in the water. The good food has made her happy, although she still doesn't actually speak. Hendrik wonders if creatures like her can talk at all. Or if they communicate using their minds, or high-pitched songs like whales, which the human ear can't hear. Ja, she's definitely on the other side of death.

So, an unexpected guest for Christmas. Family time for most people, with plenty of comings and goings; but for years now, Hendrik has gotten used to spending it completely on his own. Last night, when he discovered the creature ate kreef, so wouldn't die from hunger after all, he felt so happy that he got drunk on too much rooi and sang all the Christmas hits he could remember.

'We're having our own early Christmas party,' he told the dog, watching him sceptically from her broken basket. 'Hey, visvrou, do you believe in Jesus? Visvrou?'

The bathroom was quiet. She'd eaten plenty already, her first meal in days he imagines, and was sleeping it off. Hendrik didn't disturb her. Instead he stumbled into the bedroom, where his vroutjie's dresses still hung in Rebekkah's cupboard. He took out the yellow one with the nice flower pattern.

He doesn't make a habit of going into Rebekkah's things. He knows she won't like it. When she eventually returns to him and this cottage and their life together, she'll be furious if she thinks he's been scratching in her things. But sometimes he just can't fokken help it.

He took one of the dress sleeves and pressed it to his nose, to his lips. Then he went to the bed, unbuttoned his jeans and pushed his hand into his underpants. For the first few months after her disappearance, the dress did smell of her still. Palmolive soap. Cherry-scented shampoo. Now it all just smelt like dust. With a shudder he climaxed into his hand and fell asleep with the dress intertwined around his bare legs.

This morning he woke up, pulled up his underpants and jeans and packed the dress away. Rebekkah would never know what had happened. Afterwards, he went to go check on the water woman. She was still there, awake and waiting for breakfast. She'd made it through the night and her scales were shining brightly again. She greeted him with open, unblinking eyes and parted, smiling lips.

And she's still there. Still in his bath. She hasn't disappeared, and she eats crayfish, at least nine or ten a day, it seems, so she *must* be real. And tonight she's happy, splashing and turning in Rebekkah's bath, while Hendrik mends his traps and Jakkals snores in her basket. If I put my ear to her, Rebekkah, this visvrou of yours, will her heart sound like the sighing ocean? Like it sounds when you mos put your ear to a seashell?

He doesn't dare do that. She might bite him with those sharp little teeth of hers. Ja, he hasn't touched her again since he carried her into the house.

Hendrik gets up and flips on the electric kettle. Rebekkah loved to be in that bath too. The workers like her family, they didn't have inside baths or toilets on the farm, she told him. And not just baths – Rebekkah loved all water. She could spend hours in it. She wasn't one for the cold, though. He remembers her running the bath and also filling the kettle, lighting the blue gas flame of the stove. They still had the stovetop kettle in those days.

'I'll make tea for you,' he'd say. 'You go get in while the water's hot.'

She loved to sit in the bath and drink her tea while both were hot. He wanted her to be happy. Sometimes she'd sing. No words, just melodies. Scraps of song that maybe she'd heard on the farm. When the water had gone too cold to be pleasurable and her skin was beginning to prune, he'd hear her get up. The sound of water falling off her naked body as she stood. He'd close his eyes and imagine her stepping out – hips, small, fruity breasts, the sheen of water on her skin and black hair as she wrapped the rough towel around her. When she was dry and dressed, she'd come with a bucket and scoop out the water. Pour it onto her vegetable and flower garden. On the farm, she told him, they knew drought. She couldn't bear to see water go to waste.

''n Boer weet water is lewe,' she told him.

Ja, water is life. But it's death too, Hendrik wanted to say, thinking of all the fishermen and sailors who'd met their ends in the world's deep oceans. But he bit his tongue.

When he realised, after waiting for three months, that Rebekkah wasn't coming back to him any time soon, he couldn't bring himself to keep her garden alive. Just like that, he gave up. Now, with the drought that's hitting this region, there's no trace left of what she once made beautiful. Her hanging baskets, where she planted orange petunias and sweet tomatoes, are just dry bundles of straw that the birds raid in spring to weave their nests. Hendrik passes them as he goes outside and puts the mended trap in the tool hokkie, ready to be taken to the boat tomorrow. With all the crayfish he's suddenly catching, he needs it.

When he gets back, steam is shooting out of the kettle's spout. He takes the round tin of instant coffee. One heaped spoon. Milk, three sugars. A cloud of steam as he pours the water into the mug. Reminds him of early morning mist on the sea.

He sits down at the kitchen table and from his wallet takes out a photo, one of his favourites. It's one Rebekkah's ouma sent of Rebekkah as a teenager, standing by the dam on the plaas. She's been swimming. She's wearing an orange costume and she's laughing; but her eyes are like they often were with him, distant and hard.

Ja, the more he thinks about it, the more he's convinced that his Rebekkah has sent this darkie visvrou. It's just the sort of thing she would do. He kisses the photo and puts it back in his wallet. For five years, he's hoped, begged for a sign from his wife. Enige iets to tell him how she is and when she's coming home. So here it finally is. But what exactly Rebekkah is telling him by sending this water woman, he does not yet know.

Hendrik sips the coffee. The room's getting dark. He should get up and turn on the light, but he can't bring himself to flip the switch. The visvrou is quiet now, probably sleeping again. The only other sounds are the purring of the fridge and peaceful snoring of the dog and the drip-drip of the sink tap.

At the very bottom of the ocean, it is neither day nor night. The light from the sun or moon can only go so far down. Fish like the light, and they'll swim close to the surface in gleaming shoals, scales glinting beneath the water like strips of tinfoil. But they're also wary of it because it makes them easier prey for the circling, sea-skimming birds. In the bathroom, he imagines the water woman's silver-brown scales, glinting like a secret in the dark.

Hendrik is lying awake in bed. He can't sleep. He's polished off all the wyn in the house, but still, sleep just won't come. It must be after 3 a.m. Jakkals is snoring peacefully in her basket beside the bed. But for Hendrik there is no peace. Only memories. They've been coming through the walls like ghosts. Like the sukkel sighs of the seespoke rolling off the dark water, carried like poison into his mind.

First it's Rebekkah. All those memories of her he doesn't like thinking about. Those thoughts he fights so hard to push from his mind in the daylight. Like how, four days after Rebekkah disappeared, he went out on his boat from the place on the beach where she was last seen looking out at the ocean. He thought he glimpsed her shadow moving through the water, deep down beyond his reach, and slightly magnified, the way things look in the sea. Before he could be sure, though, it had vanished. He must've gone around and around in his boat for more than an hour after that, but he saw no further trace of her. It happened again a few days later, when he was standing on the beach at that same spot. He was looking for her, he doesn't deny it. Her body somewhere out in the water. Or even just a piece of her clothing, floating on the surface. Anything. And then he thought he saw something – Rebekkah's head and shoulders. She'd swum too far from the shore, was in trouble with the currents. Her arms were up, waving, calling, 'Help! Help!'

Tearing off his takkies and jeans, he tried to swim out to her, but the current was too strong and she kept on melting away from him. His shouting drew a curious crowd. People gathered on the beach and a tourist brought a pair of binoculars. Then some of the fishermen offloading their catches further up the beach came to help. Rolf took him out. Hendrik sat shivering in his brother-in-law's boat with a blanket wrapped around him as they circled and circled. Other fishermen joined them. But they couldn't find anything. Nothing at all.

That night, for the first time since he was a teenager, Hendrik got so drunk he pissed himself. He woke the next morning lying on his back in the dirt outside the cottage with Jakkals keeping watch.

After that, a carton of wyn became his surrogate wife and his best comfort. But it's proving useless tonight. Earlier, he went into the kitchen to find the old box cartons and cut them open for the dregs. The last dribbles tipped into his mouth, but they did nothing. He climbed back into bed. Nothing to stop the relentless tide. Rebekkah rolling in and in and in.

Hendrik takes a deep breath and tries to calm himself. To think of other things. Of how many kreef will be in the cages tomorrow. Of what he will spend the money on. I'm like a corpse that cannot find rest, he thinks to himself. And so comes Anton.

Anton in his coffin, looking almost handsome. He's wearing his navy-blue suit and his hair has been combed and gelled down. Hendrik stands in a suit too big for him, borrowed from an older cousin, peering at his brother. His brother's skin looks funny. Like it's been painted. He heard afterwards that the lady at the funeral parlour had to use a lot of makeup to hide all the bruising. And she's done Anton's hair all wrong. Anton would never part his hair like that. He wants to tell Ma, but she's crying too loudly to hear him or anyone else. 'My seun, my seun,' she sighs, before starting to cry again. When Auntie K goes to comfort her, she turns her back on the other woman like she's the enemy. Auntie K wasn't walking properly yet. Her body was still all bruised and unsteady from her time in custody. Hendrik stepped forward to offer her his arm, and she gripped him like a drowning man clinging to a life raft.

Another memory. They're sitting on a boulder overlooking the crashing ocean. Hendrik is ten, Anton fourteen. Hendrik can still feel the food they ate for Sunday lunch sitting heavy in his stomach. The modest amount of meat, sliced thin so there was enough for everyone. Carrots sprinkled with cinnamon. Rice and potatoes. Choking silence around the table, a hand around the young boys' throats. Their pa was in a kak mood, so no one dared speak. Eventually they were allowed to change their clothes and leave the house. It was like being freed from a kreef trap.

Both boys gulp in the warm sea air. Anton has brought a soccer ball, a gift from Auntie K after his good end-of-year report and the special letter from headmaster Jansen, saying if only Anton could improve his reading, he might go far. Meaning far away from their village and the life of a fisherman. Auntie K had already started taking a special interest in her eldest nephew. Although their father had yet to agree that he could join her study group.

Things Anton could do then that Hendrik couldn't. Win at soccer. Sniff out witmossels, like buried treasure. Not cry out when Pa beat him, even if he did it with a belt that drew blood. The blood would stain Anton's T-shirt or pants. Afterwards, Anton would leave the house and go for a walk, and in between the rocks where no one could see him, he'd drop his broek and wash the wounds. Hendrik didn't know if Anton allowed himself to cry then – the sting of the saltwater must've been almost as bad as the beating itself – but when his brother finally came home, his eyes were often red and puffy.

Things Anton could do. Be the first to see the boats coming in, even when they were just specks on the horizon. Tell from the men's expressions if it'd been a good or bad day out on those waters. If their iceboxes and nets were full or empty. Sneak through the fence to the light-house and avoid getting his clothes torn on the barbed wire. Spot a dassie hole or pofadder markings along the dirt roads around the village. Fillet a fish with a blade as fast as their father. Know when to tell their mother to sit down, he would make the tea or hang the washing. Mend a nylon fishing net faster than their daddy. Mend a kreef trap. In just one trip, carry everything from the shed out back to the *Lekker* down on the beach, buoys hanging around his neck, ice-chests and traps on his arms. Pluck a lekker story right out of the sea.

He turns on his side in the bed. Across the street, Mrs Simons is shouting at her husband. Earlier that day, Hendrik nearly reversed into her. She was carrying a plastic basket, on her way to hang her husband's vests and underpants to dry on the line.

'Jong Hendrik, take care! You are not the only one who lives on this street, you know ...' She straightened her doek and spat on the ground.

Had he not been in such a hurry to make his deliveries, he would've stopped the car and given her a piece of his mind. He's never liked her, even when he was a kid. She's always skinnering. Ja, she was kind at first when Rebek-kah disappeared. She brought him plates of steaming macaroni and cheese, and smoorsnoek. But after, when the weeks passed with no body and no news, like everyone else she started to think and speak the worst about his Rebekkah. That she'd left him. That she'd committed suicide by walking into the ocean, been swallowed by the ocean ghosts and would never be seen again. As Hendrik drove towards the factory, the painful memory of their rumours returned, as fresh as new cuts on his heart.

Rebekkah Anton Anton Rebekkah. Anton again – walking towards the cottage, carrying a bag of sugar their mother sent him to buy. She's baking for their sister Lattie's sixth birthday party, so it's the 7th of June 1980. Hendrik is standing outside the house. Anton is fifteen, and he's started calling Hendrik 'comrade'.

'Kom, comrade,' he'll say, 'let's go and fetch the newspaper by Karla's Kafee.'

Auntie K's got Anton into the habit of reading the newspaper. Every day she gives him the few cents for it, and after he's read it, he'll drop it at her house. This June morning, Anton has the paper under his arm. He's walking very slowly, eyes on the ground. Only when he gets very close can you see the black eye that Daddy gave him. He doesn't greet Hendrik, just gives him the bag of sugar.

'Did you buy me a Wilson's toffee?'

Anton shakes his head. 'Just take the sugar to Mommy.' His face as tight and serious as a fist.

When Hendrik comes back, Anton's sitting on the low wall. The newspaper is open and spread across his knees. There's trouble, he says; protests in the African schools across the country.

'Want to play soccer?' Hendrik asks.

Anton shakes his head again. He's got no time for soccer now, not since joining Auntie K's after-school study group. Hendrik couldn't believe it when Auntie K managed to convince their father to let Anton join. Their father was clear what Anton's future held: working the boat, catching crayfish, just like him and almost every other Coloured man in the village. But somehow she did it.

'No politics, K. I'm warning you. No Communist, UDF kak.'

'Don't you talk to me like that, little brother. I wiped your strontgat when you were a baby.'

'I mean it. Help him with his reading and his writing and sums. Maybe he'll make it to the varsity. But any politics and I won't let him go to your house!'

A few months later, Hendrik wakes while it's still dark to find that his brother's already up. He's sitting at the end of their bed, dressed and ready to go out in the boat. In the corner of the room, a candle illuminates his profile, but Hendrik can't read his brother's expression.

'Hey, wat is dit met jou? It's still early.' Groaning, Hendrik throws the covers over his head.

'I'm not going to die a fisherman. I'm going to go to varsity and I'm going to change this country. Before you finish school, there'll be plenty of books for kids like us. I don't care what Dêrra or anyone else says. I'm not scared of the Boere. I will even use a gun and kill if I have to.'

Hendrik pulls down the covers and stares through the gloom at his brother. He's shocked. Isn't killing the most terrible sin a person could do? That's what Pastor says.

Worse even than stealing, mos? Hendrik says nothing. Only swallows nervously and nods.

Later, after Anton gets accepted at the university in Cape Town, their mother takes Auntie K a cake and some meat to say thank you.

'No need for such gifts. Ons is familie. And if we don't educate the next generation, what hope is there for people like us in hierdie sieke land?'

But after Anton's death, the two women never spoke again.

'Anton, are you there? Rebekkah?'

But there's no sound except the rumble of the dog's breathing. It will be light soon. Dawn. Hendrik's not going to fall asleep. There's no point. He pulls off the covers and switches on the bedside lamp.

CHAPTER SEVEN

It's 6.30 a.m. and Hendrik's on the beach, watching the sunrise. Normally the pink blush of a new day calms him, but after the long night, he can't shake his thoughts, sour as malt vinegar.

Why does a klomp kak always happen to the good men? Anton tried to be a good man and they murdered him. With Rebekkah, Hendrik tried to be the best husband he could be, and she just got up one day and disappeared. Life throws men like Anton and himself nothing but kak, and meanwhile the skollies get away with whatever they want.

Hendrik pushes his hands into his jacket pockets and looks down the beach towards the main stretch of the village. A black man and woman are walking hand in hand towards him. The man's in a blue t-shirt and pale pink

shorts, she's all in white with a large white straw sunhat
and big sunglasses. As they pass, Hendrik hears the man
talking loudly in English on his cell phone:

'We don't hire these guys so they can—'

Probably staying in one of the rich-man hotels that
line the main beaches, Hendrik thinks. Only, how did he
make his money?

Ja, there is fokkol in common between darkies and us,
Hendrik affirms to himself, no matter what Auntie K or
Anton used to praat. If they both could see the country
now. Jirre God! Hendrik spits a gob of phlegm as the couple climb a dune, out of view. Just look at the President.
All over the newspapers, people are calling for him to go.
But like a rot you can't shift from the corks of your boat,
he stays and things only get worse. And there's no more,
'We're all blacks, fighting together for freedom and the
struggle.' Ja, Hendrik doesn't think that people like the
President even *remember* the sacrifices made by brave Coloureds like Anton and Auntie K. Since coming to power,
it's, 'Fok jou. You Coloureds had it better and we darkies
got it worse, so fok julle, we're only going to take care of
our own, now.'

Hendrik squats down on his haunches. The wet sand
feels cool beneath his palms. It'll grow warmer as the day
progresses and the sun climbs higher in the sky. He remembers being a small boy and his mommy putting him
on the ground beside her as she hung the wet bed sheets on
the line to dry. The breeze passed through them and kept
him cool. With his index finger, he scratches an A into the

sand, and next to it an R. Then he stands up and, without looking at them again, he uses his foot to kick the letters out and dusts off his hands. They're both gone, but *where*? Of course Anton's different. Anton is dood. He can visit Anton's bones in the cemetery any time he wishes. But Rebekkah … she's just keeping him waiting. And now this darkie fish woman … What does she mean, Rebekkah?

Jissus … Hendrik feels an ache in his heart. He mustn't let himself sink into despair. But sometimes he can't help it. He feels a pain, like there's a screwdriver twisting into his chest. You can pull out a rotten tooth, but you can't remove a sick heart, only make it quiet with wine and keeping busy.

Now a figure in a bright pink tracksuit is approaching from the direction of the village. He'd know that halo of frizzy orange-dyed hair anywhere. Sara. Fok, that's the *last* person he can face today. Hastily, Hendrik beats a retreat to the car park. He can hear Sara calling after him. He doesn't dare look back, but he sees from the corner of his eye that she's waving frantically, trying to get his attention.

He hasn't spoken properly with Sara in more than five years and he doesn't intend to start now. Jirre, can't that woman understand he wants nothing to do with her? Sure, they were chommies before, from when they were kids; for a long time after Anton died, Sara was the one he'd confide in. He might have even married her once, if it wasn't for all the skinner about her being a los doos. Daryll and Daryll's brother, Jerome. They both said they'd been with her by the time they were fifteen. But what really ended it for him was how Sara disappeared just when he really needed her. A week after Rebekkah vanished, when he was in a state, she up and left. Shacked up with some man, someplace else, Hendrik assumed. He didn't give it much thought. He had other things on his mind. She certainly looked thinner and more worn when she finally returned to the village and her job at the Red Sail, nearly eight months later. Her hair was cut short, too, and dyed a brassy orange. She's kept it that way ever since. But she's not a woman who can take a hint, even after all this time. When she came back to the village, she smsed him: 'Can i come see U, we need 2 talk.' When Hendrik didn't reply, she started coming to the cottage. He'd hide in the bedroom with the dog, curtains drawn, scared to breathe in case she heard. But she was no fool. She'd sit on an upturned bucket under his bedroom window with a cigarette, blowing smoke rings for him to smell.

'I can see your Toyota's here, Hendrik, and I can smell that dog of yours. Its breath stinks like rotten perlemoen. We need to talk, boetie. It's important.'

'Leave me off, Sara. I don't want to talk, voetsek!' He shouted from the bedroom.

What could she have to say to him? Unless she could tell him where Rebekkah was, he wasn't interested. She'd probably just say the same as everyone else: you must move on. Maybe she even wanted to tempt him with a bit of bodily comfort. But he was no cheat. He told himself he'd remain faithful to his wife, no matter what.

Three months ago, after five years of avoiding her, he almost pushed his trolley into Sara's at the Pick n Pay. She was inspecting bottles of hair dyes. Just in time, Hendrik dove behind a giant display of nappies.

And now here she is again, calling his name as she hurries down the beach: 'Hendrik, Hendrik!'

He gets in the car and, before Sara can reach him, he's reversed and fled.

Arriving home, he immediately locks the front door. He doesn't want to see anyone. He doesn't want anyone to cross the threshold of this cottage unless it's Rebekkah.

There are puddles of water and strands of kelp leading across the floor from the bathroom. Panicked, he hurries to the bedroom. The visvrou is sitting on his bed. She's wearing Rebekkah's yellow cotton dress. Fok …!

Where her great shining stert was just a few hours ago, there is now a pair of long, shapely legs.

CHAPTER EIGHT

THE VILLAGE PRIMARY SCHOOL houses a library, but it wasn't built by the government like Anton always promised it would be, if freedom and democracy were won. Instead, the fisheries, Church and concerned parents and villagers sponsored it. It's small, but he'll go see if there's an Afrikaans–Xhosa dictionary. Maybe if he can speak some Xhosa, this darkie visvrou will understand him and he can start asking his questions about Rebekkah.

As he walks up the path to the school behind the stone church, he remembers that first Sunday. The dogs. Rebekkah. White cotton dress. Plastic ice-cream tubs of leftovers that the braks pushed across the concrete with hungry snouts as they licked them clean.

He's left the water woman at the house. At first he didn't know what to do. Now that she has legs, she could walk out, couldn't she? But he's left his whole catch of crayfish for her, knowing that'll keep her busy. Soos 'n hond met 'n been, he thinks, and then feels angry at himself for having such a thought – why, he doesn't know, since she's mos not human. For good measure, he locked the house and brought the dog with him. He doesn't know what Jakkals might do, now that the water woman's out of the bath. What does she smell like to Jakkals? To Hendrik, she gives off no smell except the clean cool scent of ocean. Same as a freshly caught fish. But to a dog? Iets lekker om te eet? He's taking no chances. So for the moment, Jakkals is panting in the Toyota and leaving a smell like old snoek in there.

Mal, man. Locking the dog in the car so it doesn't attack the visvrou who's just grown legs and is wearing your vroutjie's dress! Fok, if anyone … Maybe I should go see the doctor, Hendrik thinks as he pushes at the school's glass doors. There's no government clinic in the village. He'd have to go to town. Anyway, he might be sick, but something is still definitely eating the crayfish, and now his wife's dress is off its hanger.

When people stepped into the house after the memorial service, there were comments.

'Get rid of the clothes. Do that quickly,' Lattie told him.

Hendrik only glowered. If he did that, what would his wife wear when she came back?

'Hendrik, you are a fokken fool. Why did you let your sister steal all my clothes?' That's what she'd say to him.

Hendrik refused to go to the service. He was tired of telling everyone that Rebekkah was coming back. Tired of explaining to people who wouldn't listen that his wife wasn't *gone* gone, just away. One day, any morning, afternoon or evening now, she'd return to him and walk into their cottage and then life would go on as before.

'It was a baie pragtige service,' his sister said. 'Children from the school read a poem and sang hymns.' Jarrad looked like he'd cried and cried and there was no sign of Michel.

Because there was no body, they couldn't have a coffin, only a blown-up photo of Rebekkah by the altar. It was taken from a class portrait – one of the teachers had arranged it at the copy shop in town. The school hosted the wake in its hall.

What was the matter with people? Hendrik wanted to scream: she isn't fokken dood, she's coming back! He felt like a piece of flotsam rolling on the ocean, no beach in sight. An empty plastic cooldrink bottle, rolling and turning. No one would listen to him.

Hendrik walks down the passage, his takkies squeaking on the freshly painted concrete. He hasn't stepped into the school since Rebekkah disappeared. Nothing seems to have changed except the walls are now pale custard yellow when before they were pale green. The lights are off and it's cool and dim inside. Along the walls are colourful drawings of faces and clouds and flowers made with cheap bright paint, with children's names underneath. Roxxy,

Grade 3. It's school holidays so the teachers aren't there, but he'll look for Principal Michaels, and if he can't find him, he'll look for Xolani.

Xolani Platjie's not a newcomer: he's one of the darkie Eastern Cape inkommers who arrived long ago, not long after Rebekkah. As handyman and caretaker, he's always at the school. He lives on the property in a little Wendy house at the back that Rebekkah arranged for him, along with the job. It will help stop the break-ins at the school, Rebekkah told the sceptical school authorities. Caretaker and free security in one. That did the trick. Before, he'd been living hand to mouth, working as a gardener for Jarrad's father-in-law and doing odd jobs here and there.

Hendrik turns right, taking the corridor that leads to the staff room and Principal's office.

'Hello? Anyone here?'

At the end of the corridor, a head pops out from around the door.

'Is Principal Michaels here?'

Xolani shakes his head, 'Everyone is home, Mr Hendrik, it's holiday time.'

'I know it's holiday time, but I was hoping ... Listen, I need a dictionary. Afrikaans and Xhosa.'

This visvrou has a message for him about his Rebekkah. He can feel it in his marrow. He must just find out what it is, that's the thing. And now he has a dictionary, he will, Hendrik thinks, looking at the thick book on the car seat beside Jakkals. Best of all, Xolani told him he can keep it until school opens again in two weeks.

'Principal Michaels will not mind,' the caretaker said. 'He lets me borrow it whenever I need it.'

The principal was once in Auntie K's study group. If there's trouble about taking the dictionary off site, Hendrik's sure he can smooth things over. In the meantime, having the dictionary at home means that Hendrik has plenty of time to get to the bottom of things. Ja, he'll soon get the answers he wants from this fish woman.

'Do you want to learn isiXhosa?' Xolani had asked.

'Ja, something like that …' replied Hendrik. What else could he tell him?

'You need a good teacher.'

At the word 'teacher', Hendrik saw Rebekkah, chalk dust marking her hands. There was always a little chalk on her clothes when she got home. He can see it, fine as flour. The children didn't have to be told to pay attention in her class. They listened because they loved her. That's what the parents and grandparents all said in their condolence cards that arrived at the cottage. There must have been at least fifteen notes written by the children too, in their messy, unsteady handwriting, "Ek huil oorlat ek jou so mis. Waarom het jy weggegaan en ons gelos? Ek wil dat jy terugkom hiernatoe." That was the note that hit Hendrik the hardest.

When he gets back to the cottage, he finds the visvrou is playing with his radio. She's turning the dial back and forth, back and forth. Hiss and crackle. Pop, gospel, jazz, talk. *Fees-must-fall-protests-on-university-campuses-across-the-country-continue-Only-yooooou-can-make-my-dreaaams-come-true-Omo-Washing-Powder* ... What will the neighbours think? What if they hear the strange racket and start their snooping? Thankfully, there are the curtains that Rebekkah put in. But if this fish woman pulls them back? If she presses her face to the window? What will Mrs Simons and the rest think – that he's given up on Rebekkah and shacked up with a darkie from the locations? Jirre God nee. The sooner he can get the truth from this creature the better.

'What do you want to say?' asked Xolani.

What *does* he want to say? Hendrik looks at the water woman. She's ignoring him. Only the radio seems to interest her. It's starting to work on his nerves, this distorted smash of voices and music as she twiddles the dial restlessly from one station to another. How are you? No, he doesn't care about that. Where have you come from? No, he's not really interested in that, either. Did Rebekkah send you? Do you have a message from her? Do you know where she is? And, most important, when is my wife coming back to me? Ja, those are his real questions.

But he can't just jump in there. Xolani told him there are rules of etiquette if you're speaking to the darkies in their own language. 'Before you ask someone their name, you should ask them how they are. It's customary,' the caretaker warned.

Hendrik squints down at the long string of words

Xolani wrote in blue ballpoint on the back of a faded airtime receipt. He's never tried to speak one of the darkies' languages before. All of them in the village mos learn Afrikaans. They have to, if they want to make a home here with the locals and find jobs. He takes a deep breath and tries:

'Unjani?'

'Once you've asked them how they are, they should ask you how you are. Then you can ask their name,' Xolani said.

Hendrik waits. But the water woman doesn't reply. Instead, she leans forward and without even looking at him turns up the volume on the radio. Hendrik must raise his voice to be heard:

'Unjarr-niii!'

He pauses hopefully and looks at the visvrou. Still nothing. No sign that she understands or has even heard him. The radio is blaring with pop, then talk, more music, talk, talk as she continues to turn the dial, station-hopping. Hendrik's begun to sweat from irritation and stress. He decides to skip straight to the what-is-your-name bit. He squints again at the scrap of paper, which is starting to crumple in his sweating fingers. He tries to say it like Xolani told him. 'Ungoobani igama lark-ho?' he practically shouts. But nothing comes from the darkie. He wishes she'd at least look at him, and turn down the fokken radio. Doesn't she know he's trying to communicate? Don't they have manners where she comes from?

Maybe if he tells her his name: 'Nnn-dingoo Hendrik.'

The visvrou yawns. Hendrik can see her small, sharp, white teeth. Then, settling back into the armchair, she closes her eyes. Sy verstaan niks nie! Maybe she's actually just dom, like bloublasies are. They always manage to get themselves beached.

He's had enough for one evening. Hendrik pushes the airtime slip into the dictionary on the table and goes to the cupboard to take out the dooswyn.

'Kom, Jakkals.' Together with the wine box, they retreat to the bedroom and close the door to block out the noise. 'Visitors in our own blerrie house.'

CHAPTER NINE

ANOTHER EXCELLENT VANGS. Thirty-eight lekker kreef fatties are now sitting in the iceboxes in the laaitjies of his boat. Hendrik can't remember when last he caught so many meaty crayfish in one go. He's glad he took the boat out. After last night, he wasn't sure he'd be up to it. Between the hangover from the wyn and lingering headache from the blaring radio that the visvrou seemed to play with until dawn, he was left feeling like a trampled dog drol. But the promise of money got him up and out on this cold sea. And here is his reward. He pats the icebakkies. It's good that this crayfish season is proving so bountiful, because the visvrou, jirre, can she eat and eat. Worse than a plaasvark. He puts the last crayfish in his iceboxes, re-baits the traps and lowers them back into the water, ready for the following day. There are still at least ten days before the tourists go back to their cities, and Hendrik plans to make as much money as he can from them before they do. If he's careful, he'll be able to save a good amount. Maybe he'll even go to town to see if there are any Christmas specials at the furniture shop. Pay nothing until Easter 2017. One of those. He could put his name down for a new lounge suite. They've never had a proper sofa, and he knows it would delight Rebekkah to find one when she comes back.

Hendrik's whistling, thinking of the new sofa to surprise Rebekkah, when he unlocks the front door. Before he opens it, he pauses for a moment. She's inside, he tells himself. It's a game of hope, of trust that he plays once or twice a month. He's going to turn the door handle, swing the door open and find ... that she has returned.

The radio's off. Batteries must have run flat. Dankie fok, Hendrik thinks as his eyes scan the room. Hoping. No, no sign of Rebekkah. But the water woman is sitting on the floor. She is holding a bundle. He stops dead in his tracks from shock.

'Jissus.'

He sees Rebekkah standing in the same place, holding that same blue blanket, six years earlier, her expression cold and closed like a steel padlock. Where has the water woman found it? Hendrik moves to take back the baby blanket that he gave to his wife as a gift all those years ago. But when he approaches, the visvrou turns her green unblinking eyes on him and from somewhere, because she doesn't actually move her lips, comes that sound, that high-pitched, piercing wail. Again, a pain, more terrible than toothache, shoots through Hendrik's entire body, from his brain down to his crotch.

'Fokken hell, visvrou!'

She squeezes the bundle tighter. Hendrik thinks his head and all his bones will explode from the pain. He grips his head and staggers backwards. The pain that's shooting through his body is unbearable. He leaves the iceboxes where he dropped them and manages to take the barking dog by the collar and drag it out. There are tears in his eyes from the pain and shock as he pulls the door shut and locks it.

Hendrik stumbles forwards, Jakkals following. His steps are automatic. His heart and head are banging. What should he do? Where are his feet carrying him? And then he knows.

Watch the stones, and the piles of earth, Hendrik tells himself as he blunders on. Some are new graves marked with simple wooden crosses. They'll only have tombstones once the families have saved, and some will never get. There are also clusters of beer bottles and cigarette stompies. Hendrik knows that teenagers come here to drink beer and smoke dagga and who knows what else.

Hendrik goes to the far right-hand corner of the cemetery, where Anton and his parents are buried. And next to them, a memorial stone for Rebekkah that others insisted on putting there. Not him. Who puts a stone down for a living woman? Hendrik falls down on his knees at the gravesides. He's a man knocked down and winded in a fight. He can feel fat tears coming now, from anger and grief. At least the pain in his head is subsiding.

'Anton, why is this happening? Anton, can you hear me?'

The cemetery is quiet. Only the rustling of the wind through the surrounding fynbos makes a noise.

'The visvrou has found the babakombers I thought Rebekkah threw away.'

Still no answer. Just silence. They will not speak to him, the seespoke, even when he needs them. They will not acknowledge his cries for help.

Meanwhile, Jakkals has stopped her barking and is moving among the graves towards the freshly dug plots. She's sniffing, squatting, pissing, leaving her pungent scent with the odours of the dead. Fokken hond. He never wanted it.

It was Rebekkah who brought the dog home, just two weeks after she told him that she'd never give him a son he could name after Anton. He'd brought her that baby blanket as a surprise. She wasn't pregnant yet. They hadn't even tried. But it was his way of saying, 'Let's start. Let's start making a family together.' But no. All he got was an ugly brak. The kind most people would just drown or shoot.

Rebekkah said she found it wandering the streets of the village. The bitch was so thirsty, it was drinking from a tidal pool. She picked it up and carried it home wrapped in her coat. The stinky hond snapped all the way, and bit

Rebekkah's hand. Rebekkah showed Hendrik a bloody thumb.

'You can't just take in any dog. Maybe it's sick.'

'Ja, she is sick. Sick of human beings,' Rebekkah said as she poured the dog a bowl of water and fed it some left-over rice and fish.

Hendrik remembers how Jakkals swallowed it down hard and fast, almost choking as she worked her jaws to get at the next bite. Later that night, when the dog was calm and fed, Rebekkah made it a place in front of the fire, on top of some sheets of newspaper and an old blanket.

'It stinks like vrot voete and it has just kakked in the bedroom,' Hendrik complained. 'It's going to make this whole place stink too.'

'I'll give her a bath, once she's learnt to trust me.'

So they were keeping it. He knew there was no point in fighting. Rebekkah wouldn't back down, now that she'd made up her mind. She was on her haunches beside the dog, which had settled by the fire. Close to it, but not so close that the dog moved. She knew not to try and stroke it. He tried to read her face, illuminated by the firelight. He couldn't believe she'd meant what she'd said just a few days earlier about never having children.

'I do not want a baby, Hendrik. Not with you or any-one. I'm not going to stop having the injection.'

She would change her mind. With time. He wouldn't push. He'd let her have the dog. In the orange firelight glow, there was something in her eyes. A look he'd come to recognise. It was the same look she got when she told him, 'I'm going for a walk,' and wouldn't let him join her. Rebekkah was there but somewhere else, her expression cold, her eyes locked doors. He couldn't reach this part of her.

Later that night, as they lay in bed, she told him she would call the dog Jakkals, same as her oupa has called his dog on the farm. Jakkals. Jackal. The sheep farmer's greatest enemy. Rebekkah had told him the story.

How every morning her oupa would get a call from the farmer over the walkie-talkie radio:

'Martin, you fokken lazy Hottentot, I can see crows! There are fokking crows. Get on your horse!'

Rebekkah's oupa knew what that meant. In the night the jackals had come down from the koppies and picked off sheep. They usually chose the old ones or the pregnant ones, or the ones who couldn't move fast enough because they were were sick or too young to fend for themselves. They ate out the liver and heart and left the rest to rot. When they got a lamb, they tore out the stomach for the mother's milk.

Jakkals. A name chosen to say fok jou to Baas Francois who her oupa despised. Jakkals. A dog imposed upon Hendrik instead of a child.

When Hendrik returns from the cemetery, he finds the visvrou sitting in his armchair in front of his television. On the screen, an African woman in a short skirt, chemically straightened hair and too much makeup is pointing to the weather chart. The blanket is still in the water woman's

arms. She's rolling and unrolling it as the weather present-
er does her smiling dance, pointing to icons representing
sun, sun and more sun over the Eastern Cape and speaking in one of the confounding darkie tongues that Hendrik
can't decode. So more drought then, Hendrik thinks. The
visvrou doesn't seem to notice Hendrik or Jakkals as they
pass into the kitchen. Hendrik can see the watery footprints she leaves wherever she goes. She'll be slowly soaking and ruining the armchair's cushions too.

Hendrik goes to the dictionary on the table and begins
to search awkwardly through its pages. The print is too
small, the words just clusters of fleas or black ants, and too
many on each page. He thinks about Auntie K's stories.
That once, the Boesman and the Xhosa tribes intermar-
ried. Hendrik hadn't paid much attention as a child or
teenager to Auntie K's political sermons. Maybe if he had,
it would be easier now to speak with this visvrou. But then,
she isn't exactly a Xhosa and he isn't exactly a Boesman.
He takes out the list of phrases Xolani has written down
for him. 'Molo unjani.' How are you. My name is …

Nee, he shakes his head, it's no good. Maybe he should
try and teach her Afrikaans. She might be better at it than
he is at the blacks' language. But he's not much of a teacher. Not like Rebekkah. Rebekkah had a gift for getting
through to even the stupidest kids; she never grew impatient with them like she did with him. He shouldn't say
stupid. Rebekkah would kak him out if she heard him use
that word. Special Educational Needs. That is what they
call dom kids these days.

Hendrik continues to search through the dictionary. He takes the pad and pencil he uses to keep track of his orders. Squinting, he eventually finds 'wife'. Inkosikazi. Only he knows that the way it's written on the page isn't necessarily how it should sound when you speak it. Who knows with these darkies and all their funny tongue clicks. Inkosikazi. He tries to speak the word clearly and confidently, but his tongue won't obey. Slowly, painfully, he finds the words for 'missing'. Then 'ocean', then 'you', then 'taken'.

The water woman turns to him. Has she finally understood something? Hope blooming, he tries again, with more gusto. But he can't shake the feeling that he's maybe just stringing a useless list of words together, like a clumsy bead necklace that any moment will snap and scatter.

Even if she does understand and replies, how will *he* understand *her*? He drops the dictionary with a thud on the table, sits down and looks at the visvrou. Then he begins to speak.

'I wanted a baby with my vroutjie. A son I could call Anton like my brother who passed. That blanket you're holding, I bought it for him. But my wife, she decided she didn't want children. She only gave me this dog instead. Do you know my Rebekkah? Do you know where she's gone? When is she coming back?'

He doesn't care whether this visvrou understands or not, or if she's even listening. It feels good just to talk. When he finally finishes telling his story, the visvrou looks at him, then drops the bundle on the floor and goes back into the bathroom.

Later on, after she's eaten her share of the crayfish and is sleeping in the bath, he picks up the cot blanket and presses it to his nose. It smells of saltwater. He locks it in the small trunk under his bed.

He returns to his armchair and, after downing half a carton of rooi as though it were no more than cooldrink, turns on the TV. He's lucky, he's missed the news. Instead, one of those 80s American movies is playing. A young, red-haired white woman in a big American city. Romantic music is playing. *Laaddddyy-in-Reeeed ... is-dancing-with-me ...*, the voice croons. Hendrik opens another carton of red wine. He doesn't bother with a glass. He gulps straight from the plastic nozzle. Lady in red ...

He places his right hand on his heart and starts to dance like they did at their wedding. The cheap red wine is making his mind spin, but he's holding Rebekkah close. She has not slipped through his fingers like sea mist. He's holding her tight, he tells himself. He sees her before him as if on their wedding day. A dress, white as sea foam, which she asked a woman in the village to make for her because she wanted the day to be sommer perfect. He sees himself in the kerk hall, a little tipsy after the speeches, his leather shoes polished until they look brand new. Everyone is watching and he wants to get this right. And he thinks he has. Rebekkah is happy. Laughing. The DJ plays the song he requested, to surprise her. *Lady-in-Red ... is-dancing-with-me ...* Her ouma and oupa are there and it's good to finally meeting them. To see where she's come from, to finally meet her people as she's met his.

Hendrik pulls his bride closer. There's only the two of them now. Not the visvrou. Not Jakkals, the pavement special. Just the two of them. And everything is perfect.

Only this is not how it happened. They married in the registry office. She wanted no friends there, no family. And it turns out she never even told her ouma or oupa. The registry supplied the witnesses, two clerks who kept their IDs with them for such occasions. She wore a normal dress, although she put a white rose in her hair. When they drove home, Hendrik with his hand on her knee, he suggested they go to a restaurant in the village. Not the Red Sail. Someplace else. Maybe the one built right on the beach next to the reserve entrance. It was extravagant, he knew. Coloured villagers like them never went to the overpriced restaurants that catered to tourists.

She shook her head. 'Too expensive.' Pay day was still three weeks away and they'd paid for the marriage licence. And why must he insist on making such a fuss?

'Take me to the beach,' she said. 'I want to see the waves.'

So that's where they went.

'Dance with me,' Hendrik asked.

He pulled her close and pushed his cheek against hers.

'I love you,' he whispered. 'You make me so happy. My pragtige vroutjie.'

But he could feel her stiffen as he moved her, without music, in circles on the sand. She only lasted three or four turns before she gently unlocked his arms and stepped away. Without a word, she turned her back on him, and watched the setting sun dissolve into the ocean like a Disprin tablet. Later that night, he'd tip the sand out of his shoes.

CHAPTER TEN

HENDRIK IS ON THE BEACH. It is pre-dawn and all he can see is darkness. Black sky, black beach, black ocean. A cold wind is whooshing off the water, whipping up the sand so that it stings his arms and irritates his eyes and makes the seespoke complain even louder than usual with their lisping howls and moans. He's drunk every last drop of rooi in the house and still his mind is whirling like a fokken windduiwel. Angrily he shouts Rebekkah's name, once, twice, three times. Nothing. No reply. Okay, so she wanted to disappear, but could she not have given him a boy first, so that he would have some company until she felt ready to come home? Unless ... He can feel that agony of doubt gathering in him again, and with it a rising panic. There's the sour taste of fear in his mouth. Nee, he must not think like this. 'Rebekkah is coming back!' he screams at the waves. The seespoke sigh back, but Hendrik knows they only think of their own problems. By the time he returns shivering with cold to the cottage, he has mos made up his mind.

He lures the visvrou out of the bath and into the car with a stunned crayfish. Pieter, Rolf and the others won't be on the beaches yet. They'll be waiting for the wind to die down before deciding whether or not it's safe to take their bakkie boats out. He'll drive her back to the cove where he found her, deserted in weather like this, and he'll send her on her way. This visvrou must sommer piss off. Ever since she came into his life two weeks ago, he's been chased by gutting memories and thoughts. Before, with a little help from the soet rooi, they were under control, but now they're stamping their muck all over his brain like a herd of filthy beasts let loose.

In the car, the water woman strokes the dashboard, then with a look of disgust bangs the plastic with her fist. Jirre, Hendrik thinks as he turns on the engine and backs out of the yard. Good to get rid of her.

When they reach the cove, Hendrik parks the car and gets out to open the door for the visvrou. He's prepared to drag her into the icy waters if he has to, but she walks straight down to the rolling surf, feet crunching over the break line of sea shells and plastic refuse. Hendrik scrambles onto a large boulder that overlooks the cove, and watches. The visvrou walks into the icy frothing water still wearing Rebekkah's dress. Hendrik flinches. Rebekkah will want to know what happened to that dress when she comes home. Still, it's a small price to pay to be rid of this creature.

The ocean is calmer than it was earlier, but the oncoming breeze means it's still choppy. Ankles, calves, thighs. Rebekkah's yellow dress balloons up around the visvrou. Then she dives down and is gone. At what point her legs become a tail again he doesn't know, but by the time she's fifty metres out he can see it moving beneath the water with all the easy elegance of a dolphin's.

He turns to go, but something makes him linger. Her shape, rising in and out of the water, has suddenly changed direction.

Wag. Hendrik squints. She's swimming back towards the village!

He scrambles up a larger outreaching boulder so that he's standing right over the waves. He begins to yell and flap as sea spray smashes up against him – more than once, still woozy from the wine, he almost loses his balance.

'Fokken darkie … *die* pad!' He jabs furiously in the direction that would lead her out to open sea and out of his life. She's moving in circles now, with one tail fin up out of the water like a shark's. A realisation pops into Hendrik's mind. This darkie visvrou is lost! She's dithering because she doesn't know which way is home.

Oh jirre. For a moment, Hendrik considers going to fetch his boat and coming back via the water to guide her. A seagull shoots past, its wing tips grazing the water, its mouth full of 'caw caw!' He imagines the visvrou panting with exhaustion. The choppy waves have confused her, swirling her inner compass like sand on the ocean floor. Nee. She must mos figure it out for herself, or her lot must come and get her. Hendrik jumps back into the car. Locks the doors and screeches off.

When he returns to the cottage, Jakkals is lying on her side in the sunshine, white and curly as sea foam. He pats the dog's head as he steps past, but Jakkals bares fangs and gives a low growl.

'Fine, you can go too.' Ja, no question, he's the one who wears the broek. The one who decides what is what. And now that the visvrou is gone, the cottage belongs to them again, to him and his Rebekkah. He begins to whistle. He'll make himself a lekker cup of coffee and a polony sandwich. With a sense of relief, he turns the doorknob.

But as soon as he steps inside, he notices the puddles leading from the front door. Some are marked with strands of fresh, slimy seaweed. In disbelief, Hendrik follows them to the bathroom. The visvrou has returned to the bath! It isn't possible, but somehow she's done it. When Hendrik flicks on the light, there she is in the water, still wearing Rebekkah's dress. She turns to look at him, but he doesn't dare to catch her eye. Outwitted by a fokken fish woman! What is he supposed to do now?

CHAPTER ELEVEN

THE VISVROU IS IN THE BATH, snoring as loudly as a diesel engine. Bubbles of spittle form on her purple lips with each long exhale, and her arms hang limply over the sides. She's utterly exhausted, it seems, after her swimming ordeal. Hendrik's been watching her a long time, since she fell asleep. It's true, he finds it hard to look at the creature for too long when she's awake. To really scrutinise her. Partly because he's been frightened she might take offence and let out another of her groin-shattering screams. But now that she's sleeping, and he's probably stuck with her for the time being, he does look. This is what he sees.

She has the figure of a young woman. Her breasts are still firm and pert, her hips are narrow. Her dark skin is smooth, with no sign of wrinkles on her face or stretch marks on her thighs and stomach. She looks maybe twenty-six, twenty-seven. Less than thirty. Although maybe it's not the same with a visvrou. Maybe she is ancient, like the sea itself. That never actually looks old, only sick when humans dump all their oil and kak in it. Her black hair is short and curled tightly, not long and flowing like when you see mermaids in picture books. He doesn't think it's grown at all since she arrived. Her nails are short too. Her feet are pink underneath and the skin looks soft, like a baby's. Hendrik steps closer to look at the foot dangling over the bath. Yes, the sole is wrinkled. But it could be from all the time she spends soaking in the bath, rather than because she hasn't walked on them much yet. Her mouth is small, her lips the colour of plum jam. Her teeth, he can't see her teeth. But he knows from those times when she's screamed, or torn into the kreef, or smiled that they're pointed and sharp like a fish's. And small. Her nose … Is just a nose. His eyes travel down. He can see the outline of her koek, which looks like it's hairless beneath the wet fabric of Rebekkah's dress. There's no hair on this visvrou anywhere, except for on her head. She doesn't even have eyelashes or eyebrows.

Her eyes … They're closed now, but it's her eyes that strike Hendrik the most. Not just their colour, but the fact that their expression is so difficult to read. When he has had the courage to look into them, it's like staring into the gently trembling ocean. You can't see to the emotion at the bottom. At times, this has made Hendrik afraid. You can tell what a dog is thinking immediately. A cat.

Even a bird. But he can't tell what this visvrou is thinking. Like a fish, she never blinks, just keeps her green oë fixed on you, like she knows what you're going to do or say before even you do. Thinking about it sends jelly shivers along Hendrik's spine and into his toes.

He leaves the bathroom. He must sober up, now that the wind's died down and it's safe to go out on his boat. All he really wants to do is crawl into bed and feel the warm sunlight falling through the bedroom window onto his face. To lie there like a lazy, dozing cat, without a worry in the world. But he has a whole new list of Christmas orders to fulfil. Just like his catches, for some reason, business has never been better. He doesn't even have to look for customers, dangling bags of crayfish in front of passing motorists. They're coming to him.

When he's been paid, he'll drive to Pick n Pay in town for the weekly shop. Then he'll go see Xolani again. The caretaker will probably be off to the Eastern Cape soon. That's one thing Hendrik knows about the darkies: they go back to the Transkei this time of year to be with their families. But he saw the caretaker just yesterday, walking past the Red Sail pub. He's surprised Xolani hasn't gone already, but maybe Principal Michaels asked him to stay a bit longer to keep an eye out for skollies wanting to break into the deserted school. Anyway, Hendrik wants to catch him before he goes and ask him some more questions. Maybe Xolani knows something that can help Hendrik either finally communicate with, or rid himself of, this darkie visvrou. Hendrik swallows another mouthful of hot coffee and pours what's left into his flask. Okay. Now he can manage. He gathers his rucksack, locks the cottage and walks down to the beach.

Where did Rebekkah disappear to, those nights when she wasn't at home? This question used to torture Hendrik when they were first getting to know one another, sommer net chommies. He knew from his spying that some nights the lights were off when he drove past her place and it was still too early for her to be asleep. He began to worry that she had a lover. The thought made him sick to his stomach. He had to find out the truth. So he asked Lattie – who knows everyone's business, you fart and she smells it – and Jarrad, who seemed to know Rebekkah the best.

But Lattie said she had no idea; the less she knew about Rebekkah, the happier she was. And Jarrad just shrugged, 'Listen, Oom, she and I hardly speak. I'm not the person to ask.'

That afternoon, Rebekkah phoned him.

'I hear you've been worrying because I'm not in my cottage some nights. I like to go down to the beach for walks by myself. I don't like it that you're skinnering about me, okay?'

So Jarrad told her! Fok, that's the last time he'd go to his dikgat nephew with his troubles.

'Ja-nee, I was just concerned, as your friend …' Hendrik tried to keep his tone casual, but his sentence trailed off.

He tried to persuade her to at least wait until dawn, when fishermen like him were around. The village isn't as safe as it once was, he told her, and she was still new to it, still an inkommer – even though she'd been living in the community for almost six months by then.

'Young people are getting up to all kinds of mischief, Rebekkah. And there are darkies now and the nakkas who might, you know, rape you … And the tik addicts. They'll steal anything.'

But she told him firmly, 'I can look after myself. Don't tell me what to do, okay Hendrik?'

Ja, nobody was allowed to tell Rebekkah anything. That woman was stubborn. One afternoon after work, when he went to visit her in her cottage, he found her sitting on a chair, dabbing the heel of her foot with Dettol. There was a trail of bloody footprints through the house. She'd stepped in glass. There's often glass hidden in the sand these days – broken bottlenecks, dangerous as daggers. Still, on their beach jaunts together, sometimes Rebekkah took a blanket to wrap around her shoulders or to sit on, but never shoes.

When he asked her why not, she explained, 'We didn't wear shoes on the farm. Only on Sundays when we went to church. Ouma made me scrub my feet with carbolic soap before I put them on, to keep them clean. It felt strange and I felt important. The shoes made me walk slowly, not fast, like the other days. But I never got used to them. It was only at varsity that I wore shoes every day for the first time in my life.'

What did she look like when she was just a girl with no shoes, hunting for mermaids on the farm? He couldn't see her as anything but his Rebekkah. Tall and thin; long, dark hair, mostly tied back. The large scar on her inner thigh, shaped like a sickle moon, which he saw once when they went swimming and she was drying herself off. How did she get that? And teaching college? What was she like then? He considered asking Jarrad, but he didn't want his sister's son to know any more of his business.

After Rebekkah cut her foot, he bought her a pair of flip-flops. But she gave the parcel back.

'It's not a romantic gift. It is a friend gift, okay?' His voice sounded frustrated, although he didn't want it to.

She laughed, and this time accepted the shoes. But he knew she wouldn't use them, and would walk barefoot again down the beach paths. In the morning there'd be sand on the floor of her cottage, and when he drove past on his way to his boat he'd see her, dressed for school, sweeping it out of her front door.

When Hendrik gets down to the beach, most of the fishermen are already out. Daryll is sitting in his 4×4 having a smoke.

'Môre, Hendrik. Late night?'

'Ja, something like that.'

Daryll helps Hendrik clip the tow rope onto *Lekker*. Lionel and Rolf are on the beach too. 'Môre-môre, Hendrik,' they greet him. 'Be careful out there. Someone thinks they spotted a great white.'

'Is hulle seker?' Sharks are rare in these icy Atlantic waters. They prefer the warmer waters towards the Cape and beyond, as the Indian Ocean seeps in.

'Ja, a few hours ago.'

Hendrik thinks about the visvrou, swimming too close to the shore that morning. He nods and climbs into his boat and pulls the motor.

When he gets to his traps, he can't believe his luck. Full to bursting, even the extra ones he baited yesterday. He'll need to buy more ice chests to store them in, and find more customers.

CHAPTER TWELVE

THE SUPERMARKET LOOKS like someone has come and shat Christmas all over it. Everywhere you look there's tinsel and twinkling lights, and over the airwaves nothing but Christmas hits.

Jissus. Hendrik pulls out a trolley. He passes a young man with bad skin stacking shelves with bottles of All Gold tomato sauce, which the bright poster says are on x-mas special. Hendrik supposes they teach them to stack cans and bottles like that. Labels facing outwards, neat as soldiers. Must get boring. He'd be tempted to make mischief.

Hendrik pushes his trolley past the condiments and turns right towards the wine aisle. In his jacket pocket is more than nine hundred rand in twenties, fifties and hundreds, the most he's ever made for a single catch. There were enough crayfish in his baskets this morning to fill three icebakkies. After he mentally deducted the visvrou's, he still had plenty. Would he sell them all? But he was hardly off his boat when his cell phone started to ring. He fumbled in his pocket, his finger joints still stiff from the cold water.

It was Kobus from the Dancing Mussel restaurant. He wanted an extra twenty-three. A large group of German tourists had just made a last-minute booking. Hendrik looked down at his icebox. It was exactly how many extra he'd caught. Ja, he can't remember when last he had so much business. Every day someone else seems to stop him in the street, asking if he has any crayfish for them. On his way to see Kobus, Mark and his wife stopped their car next to his.

'Hey, Hendrik, where did you get those crayfish from? Freshest and best I've ever tasted, man. We have friends coming for the weekend. Do you think you can manage fifteen more?'

Hendrik just nodded and agreed to drop them off that Thursday, Christmas Eve.

In his mind, he runs through the list of orders accumulating for the holiday weekend. Fifteen for Mark and his rich white friends flying in from Pretoria. Thirty for one restaurant. Twenty-seven for another. And there's still his regular quota for the factory. Where's he supposed to catch them all? He hasn't worked this hard since he was a boy, taking over from Anton on their father's boat. By then Anton was busy with his studies at the University of the Western Cape.

Hendrik would sit in the boat, teeth chattering, the light bouncing off the ocean as bright as a blade, while his father, still stinking of the previous night's beer dompies, sat at the stern in his yellow waterproofs and steered the speeding bakkie off shore. He'd think of Anton in his nice, warm university library. Anton had written to tell him about it. Walls and walls of nothing but boeke, and you were meant to read them. Hendrik felt jaloers, ja, he can admit that now.

Hendrik turns his trolley into the wine section. Which should he take? He wants to try something good, something that comes in a glass bottle, not the usual dooswyn. He looks at the labels. They sound like women's names: Shiraz, Merlot, Chardonnay. How are you supposed to know what's decent? By the price?

Not to have to worry about the prices. To buy without mentally calculating how much you've already spent, and what little is left. That's a rich man's life, he always thought as a boy, watching some of the whites shop. The tourists and the local farmers. They filled their trolleys without even looking at the prices, loading in bulging braai packs of lamb, boerewors, steak and large bottles of cooldrink. Every day on their tables it was like Christmas.

He wishes Rebekkah was experiencing this with him. Ja, he's feeling better again. He'll show her how much he loves her, has never stopped loving her, even after what she's done to him. With all this new cash, he'll spoil her rotten when she comes home to him. Not that they were poor. With her modest salary as a teacher and his crayfish and snoek catches, they didn't have it bad. And if he ever had an extra twenty or fifty in his pocket, he always brought her home a little gift. Sometimes just a slab of her favourite fruit-and-nut chocolate, but always something. There were others who had it worse. And they didn't want much. Just each other. But until she comes back to him, he wants everything else. Good food and wine. Maybe even brandy too. Hendrik decides on two bottles of wine and puts them in the trolley. He smiles to himself as he pushes the trolley towards the meat.

By the chips and biscuits, Hendrik sees Villeen, Sara's eldest sister. She's with her young grandchildren. Sara's other sister still lives by Cape Town. The two little girls are tugging at Villeen's sleeve as she puts back on the shelf the biscuits they tried to slip into her trolley. Hendrik hangs back. Siestog, Villeen looks drawn and thin as a slice of that brittle melba toast they serve in the hotels. A year ago, she chose to retire from the crayfish factory early. He heard her talking about it: 'Ek is moeg. I want to spoil myself for a change.'

She'd worked at the factory for forty years, since she was seventeen, and took her entire pension, three hundred thousand rands, as a one-shot pay-out. It was the talk of the village. Immediately the spending started. First, a special trip down to Cape Town, which she'd never visited before, to buy new clothes. Her three daughters joined her and they all got new wardrobes too.

'It looks like someone went and robbed Woolworths with all those bags,' he heard Mrs Simons gossiping, sourly.

Then Villeen bought a 28-inch flat-screen TV and a dishwasher. She called in Billie and his crew to redo her kitchen. Bought her favourite son, a useless skollie of nearly thirty who never does anything but smoke dagga on Wine Hill and make girls pregnant, a motorbike.

Four months later, the money was all gone. Two weeks ago, he saw someone coming to pick up the motorbike. He heard Villeen tried to get her old job back at the factory, but it was filled. Now she's forced to do piecemeal char work for a self-catering cottage when they have guests.

For a second, he thinks of going back and stuffing a few hundred rands in her pocket. Tell her it's for the grandkids. But he thinks better of it. What if she's insulted? Worse, what if Sara gets to hear about it? He doesn't want to encourage her or let her think that he's forgiven her. And people might skinner. Rebekkah might come back and hear rumours. Jissus, people in the village can skinner. It is like a disease. But he should probably save some of the money to give Xolani a little something. Hendrik doesn't want to feel indebted.

When Hendrik gets home from the supermarket, he carries the bags inside. He can feel Mrs Simons and her daughter-in-law watching. Their money will be tight now, after all the pre-Christmas presents and splurging, and they're probably wondering where he got his from. It's a long time since they last saw him able to afford so many things from Pick n Pay. Goed so, hulle kan ma' kyk! He's sure that for years they've thought him useless.

Anton was the son who was really going to make something of himself. Well, now Hendrik's luck is turning, so let them look and skinner until their tongues drop off from all their wagging.

The water woman is dozing in the armchair. He dumps the bags beside the sink and ignores the dog, who is already up, snuffling the air because of the meat.

He takes out one of the new bottles of wine. He chose this one because he liked the golden tree with gnarled, reaching branches on the label. He twists open the top and pours himself a large glass. Without sitting down, he swirls the red wine in his mouth. Not bad, this pricy stuff. But he must go and see Xolani and take back the dictionary, which hasn't fokken helped at all. He's about to swallow the last few mouthfuls of red when he sees it. Rebekkah's handbag. The water woman has tipped its contents out on the kitchen table.

He sees Rebekkah walking past him early one morning as he sits at that table, spreading peanut butter on a slice of bread. I'm going to work early, she says without looking at him. She has extra preparation to do. The handbag swings on her shoulder and he thinks he can see the end of a swimming costume sticking out of it.

'What are they learning?' Hendrik calls after her.

The door bangs. No answer.

Hendrik hasn't gone near the handbag since the police came and asked to look at it, after Rebekkah had been missing for more than seventy-two hours. The uniformed cop listed the items for the plainclothes cop to write in his report. That one in normal clothes was Daryll's cousin. Hendrik sees him around all the time. It's like that in this community. No one is far from anyone else in terms of blood, unless they're inkommers like Rebekkah.

Lattie was also there, boiling the kettle and preparing tea. She brought out a plate with Marie biscuits on a doily. Then they all sat at this same table, and one by one examined and recorded the items. Cell phone. Lipstick. Chalk, three sticks. One brand new. Always teacher's chalk in her bag, she kept it in a small ziplock bag. Red pen for marking. Strip of gold star stickers to reward the learners whose work improved. Brown leather purse, with money, ID book and bank cards still in it. House keys. Other keys.

'Those must be her school keys,' Lattie piped up.

'School keys,' the policeman repeated. Daryll's cousin wrote it down.

Rebekkah won't like this, Hendrik thought. He could feel Lattie craning her neck to have a snoop.

He was feeling very irritable towards his sister, even though she'd come to the cottage to help tidy up before the police came around. 'They're not the fokken pastor!' he'd wanted to shout as Lattie fussed over how much milk each policeman wanted. Then she started washing up. Three days' worth of mugs, glasses, pots and plates. Hendrik had had no intention of doing any of it until Rebekkah came home. When she does, he thought, she'll see what a mess this game of hers has left him in. And then Lattie wanted to take the spare set of keys back to the school, and they had a fight about it right there in front of the two embarrassed policemen.

'Don't touch Rebekkah's things!'

'But those keys must go back to the school. They are private property.'

'She'll need them when she comes back.'

'I'm taking them, Hendrik.'

Lattie reached forward to snatch them off the table, but Hendrik was too quick for her.

The two policemen just watched.

'Apologise!' Hendrik bellowed, clutching the keys to his chest.

'Vir wat? Nee! She's never coming back, and those keys must be returned to the school!'

'Apologise!' Hendrik screamed even louder, tears streaming down his face.

'Neeee! She is never coming back – and you know what? I for one am happy she's gone! She was only trouble since she came to this village, and you're lucky to be rid of her.'

Hendrik's head slumped onto the table and he began to sob uncontrollably. He heard the policemen stand up and excuse themselves as Lattie let them out.

'Apologise. Say it isn't true ...' Hendrik cried, more feebly now.

'Neeeee! Ek sallie,' Lattie hissed, and Hendrik heard her slam the door.

Their relationship was never the same after that. As time went on, they spoke less and less, until they stopped speaking altogether.

Maybe he was too hard on her. His sister had seemed very nervous that morning with the policemen in the house. She was just a girl the last time police invaded this place, voices booming off the walls, bursting doors and hearts off their hinges. Those blerrie bastards. His mother only just had time to put a coat over her nightdress and Pa's knitted hat over her stocking-covered hair before she and the others were pushed outside to shiver in the dark while dirty boots crashed through the rooms. Cushions were torn open, sponge stuffing scattered and Anton's suitcase confiscated. And then the terrible questioning began. Their pa had already had his stroke and was by the hospital. His ma looked like her eyes would pop from her head with terror. He was fifteen. He thought his ma might drop dead from fear and he was not ready to be an orphan.

Later, the family heard that the police had taken Auntie K, too, when they arrested Anton and his varsity friends who were staying by her place.

With trembling hands, Hendrik picks up the wine and takes a gulp. His vroutjie is a neat woman. She's not the sort to have her handbag bursting with old snot-rags and useless kak. She won't like having her things scattered all over the table like this, even if a visvrou did it.

He picks up Rebekkah's cell phone, pushes the power button. Dood. It hasn't been charged for five years, so it's not a surprise.

'Why did you take all these things out, visvrou? What are you trying to do?'

Xolani unlocks the door of his Wendy house when Hendrik bangs on it. 'I'm sorry. There are some important things I need to ask you.'

For a moment, the caretaker stands looking at Hendrik with a frown of surprise. But then his expression changes and he invites Hendrik in as though he's been waiting for him. Outside in the dark, the village simmers with the sounds of tourists laughing and shouting in a nearby pizza bar.

Hendrik's never been inside Xolani's house before. Once, he helped Rebekkah carry an old mattress here for him, and the gift of a folding camping table that had once belonged to Auntie K, but he's never actually been inside. The Wendy house is small. No more, Hendrik calculates, than two and a half by three metres – really, not a lot bigger than *Lekker*. But it's not crowded or messy. Everything seems to have its ordered place. One whole wall is taken up with the mattress on wooden pallets on the floor. The bed is neatly made, a blue and black blanket thrown over it. Above the bed there's a shelf with a stack of books neatly piled on it. A suit hangs from a small folding cloth wardrobe that covers the far window. The camping table and two chairs are against the wall opposite the bed, and under the other window, to Hendrik's left when he walks in, a small table with a two-point burner and an enamel basin. There's a pot of steaming pap on the stove and another pan with some spinach.

Xolani was about to eat dinner. Fok, should he go? But before Hendrik can say anything, Xolani clears a space for him at the table, telling him to sit as he goes to the pots, takes another plate and serves Hendrik a generous helping. He slices them each a thick piece of soft white bread, too, and puts them on the plates with the pap and spinach. The food is steaming hot and smells delicious. Hendrik realises he hasn't eaten since breakfast. They eat in silence. Xolani doesn't seem troubled by it. Occasionally he looks out the window into the schoolyard like a man who is remembering.

When they've both finished, Xolani stands up and takes the two plates and puts them in an enamel basin in the kitchen area. Then he lights the gas again and put the kettle on.

'Coffee?'

Hendrik nods.

Xolani takes two enamel mugs down from the shelf. While the kettle's boiling, he returns to his seat and offers Hendrik a cigarette from the packet in his shirt pocket. Hendrik shakes his head. Xolani lights his, shakes out the match and puts it carefully back into the matchbox.

'All right, Mr Hendrik, what are the questions you must ask?'

Hendrik shifts awkwardly in his chair. The questions which had made him leave the house so abruptly, and drive here to knock on Xolani's door for the very first time, seem less urgent now. But still, there are things he needs to know, secrets about these visvrouens that he's sure only darkies like Xolani know, so since he's with Xolani, he will ask.

'Do you know any stories … I mean, did you ever hear any stories about fish women?'

Once again Xolani looks surprised, like this was not what he was expecting. 'Fish women,' he repeats slowly. 'Is that the important question you have come here to ask?'

'Ja, I know. It's a strange question, but something has happened and I need to know.'

Hendrik's relieved when Xolani doesn't ask what has happened. If nothing else, this darkie is discreet. When Rebekkah disappeared, he was one of the few who didn't ask what or when or how, or even offer his condolences – not even when, one afternoon about five months after Rebekkah went, he arrived at Hendrik's cottage with a box of Rebekkah's personal possessions from the school. He just left the box on the doorstep and slipped away. Hendrik watched him go from behind the curtain in his bedroom.

'Fish women?' Xolani repeats, sucking again on his cigarette.

'Ja, you know, black women who are normal from here to here, but vis from here to here.' Hendrik points to his waist. 'Except,' Hendrik adds, 'they can grow legs too, if they want.'

'Oh, ja. But I never heard about them in Port Elizabeth where I lived. Only in the Transkei, in my gogo's village.' A soft cloud of smoke escapes Xolani's nostrils. 'My gogo said they come with the Fortune Snake. I've never seen one myself, but mamlambo is what they are called. That is what the old people say.'

'Mamalamboo?'

Xolani laughs as he gets up to take the rattling kettle off the heat. Hendrik watches as Xolani prepares two mugs with Ricoffy, stirring in two teaspoons of sugar and some milk that he takes from the tiny bar fridge. 'Mamlam-bo. She is a special creature who brings her owner great fortune, but always at a heavy price. She is jealous and possessive. She will not share him with others. You can buy them from the igqirha.' Xolani pours the boiling water. 'Maybe I should get one. Then I would be a wealthy man.' He laughs again, shaking his head as he passes Hendrik his mug.

Sipping their coffees, they fall back into silence. Xolani finishes his cigarette and puts it out under his shoe, then places the stompie in a jar under the table. Hendrik's mind, though, is very noisy. He knew it. His Rebekkah must have sent him this visvrou to help him until she returns. Hendrik feels so excited, he can hardly sit still. His Rebekkah knows about such things, and knows how hard life has been for him since she went. She maybe even feels guilty or wants him to know she's thinking of him. She's sent this water maiden to bring him money, so that maybe he can even save some money before she returns. He should go back and ask the visvrou herself. Now that he knows what she's called. But first, Hendrik puts down his mug and takes a fifty rand from his pocket.

'This is for you, Xolani. For the food – and you've been helping me—'

Xolani puts down his cup of coffee. His smile is gone and his voice sounds hurt: 'Haai, no man. Your wife was very good to me. She helped me to find this job and my accommodation here. Please, I don't want your money.'

Hendrik nods. 'What are you reading?' he asks, pointing to the shelf above Xolani's bed.

Xolani shrugs, his unhappy expression gone. 'Principal Michaels has lent them to me. Some politics, some literature, some history and even one book of poems. I am trying to enrich this intloko of mine,' Xolani points to his head and laughs, 'but I fear it may be too late.'

The visvrou is still awake and sitting at the kitchen table when Hendrik returns from Xolani. Rebekkah's handbag is gone. Presumably she's put it back in the cupboard. Instead she now has a pile of her T-shirts and jerseys on the table in front of her.

'Mam-lam-bo, did my Rebekkah send you to me to make me rich?'

He says it slowly. He tries to pronounce it exactly like Xolani did, but he knows he's not saying it right. Hendrik picks up a jersey. A pale grey one that she liked to wear to work.

'My vroutjie Rebekkah, she liked this one. It was her favourite.'

The water woman turns her face and settles her eyes on him. Like looking into dark, deep, bottle-green water. The kind you find in a harbour. The activity below is hidden. You can only see what's floating on the surface.

Her eyes follow him as he goes to the fridge. Where's that wine he bought earlier at the supermarket? He feels strangely calm, even happy. He will not give up hope. If Rebekkah loves him enough to send him a mam-lamb-ding, he thinks, pouring the wine and taking a sip, it's only a matter of time before she comes herself. Whistling to himself, he inspects the fridge. For the mam-lamb, five crayfish. For himself? Ja, that pap and spinach dinner with Xolani was nice, but he still feels hungry. He can have chops for supper every night this week if he wants, and real butter on his bread too. He puts both by the stove and reaches for the pan that he forgot to wash yesterday. The fat's congealed inside, white as melted wax, but so what. He lights the gas. Meanwhile the visvrou is playing with Rebekkah's makeup. She's tipped the eyeshadow onto the table and is pressing the compressed pink powder with her fingers so it crumbles like dried paint.

He pours himself another glass of wine and, looking at the water woman, declares: 'Ek drink op jou, my Rebek-kah. To you.'

The visvrou pays him no attention. Hendrik shrugs and turns back to the pan, which is smoking slightly, ready for the meat. He will have both chops, he decides. The meat sizzles. Another gulp of wine. He smacks his lips. It is lekker wyn. Smooth. Not hard as sandpaper on the palate, like the dooswyn. He whistles as he flips the meat over. So his wife has sent him a goue gans. Thanks to her, his skip het ingekom. He swallows another mouth-ful of wine. Ha. Soet vroutjie. He can feel the water wom-an is watching him. He pours another glass. Gulps it. He's starting to feel tipsy, and with it the heaviness is lift-ing even more from his heart.

Still she watches him. Something about it makes him uncomfortable, and he goes to sit in the armchair with his back to the table, the plate of chops and buttered bread resting on his lap and the bottle of wine next to him. Jakkals is waiting at his feet for her share. He can hear the water woman playing with the tin opener. Click click click. Hendrik gets up and turns on the television.

Oh Jissus, die 9 o'clock slegte nuus. Again blacks are talking. Again pictures of the President's new rural homestead, this one in the Eastern Cape. A huge development with diggers and lorries rolling around and causing clouds of dust. What's going on now? He knows it must have something to do with corruption. Last month, spoilt students rioting on university campuses. This month, Mr President's new blerrie holiday house. Country is going down the kakpipe. He stretches forwards to change channels. *SA's got Talent* is on SABC 2. He wants to see what's become of the little brother and sister ballroom dancing combo, and the woman who can bend her body like a piece of putty.

Suddenly the visvrou woman is standing behind him. He can smell her, salty and pungent like summer seawater. He whips round. She's leaning over his chair, peering at the screen. Then she starts to sway like seaweed in water. She opens her mouth, but nothing comes out except a damp, sucking sound. Then it comes, the terrible waterwoman howl … the pain! It shoots through Hendrik and he drops the plate of meat and spills the delicious wine.

CHAPTER THIRTEEN

SOMETHING ON TELEVISION has caught visvrou's attention. Something to do with the news. Hendrik never watches the news these days if he can help it. And he never reads the paper now either. All you have to do is drive and see the headline boards to feel you don't want to know more. Ja, the only news these days is kak nuus. So why is visvrou so interested? Or do her sort have an appetite for blood and crime?

Last night, for the first time, once her howling had stopped, the visvrou did not return to the bath but slept in his armchair instead. She wouldn't let him turn off the television. She wouldn't let him near it. Each time he tried, she opened her mouth, showing her sharp teeth, as if warning him of another scream. He backed off and locked himself in the bedroom, and lay awake much of the night, aware of the television's non-stop noise. In the dark, its electric blue light made the visvrou's skin shine, as though once again she had her tail and scales. Jakkals slept at the visvrou's feet, not seeming to mind the small puddle that always appears when she stays in one place for a long time. Both were still snoring when Hendrik woke and crept out of his bedroom. He tiptoed past them and the TV, still on, carrying his ice chests and rucksack. He didn't stop to brush his teeth or wash his face at the kitchen sink, or even make himself a piece of buttered bread and a cup of coffee. He didn't want to wake this visvrou in case she conjured one of her tooth-searing, silent shrieks. He felt like he wouldn't survive it.

Now he's home again, and things are much as expected. The visvrou hasn't moved. Around the armchair, strands of seaweed and kelp are drying out and turning white with salt. On the news, the newsreader is reporting about Mr President. Something about a sacred river estuary diverted for his special country retreat. Just shut up, Hendrik thinks, frustrated, as he staggers past with his ice chests all stuffed to bursting with fat and lively kreef.

For once, the water woman doesn't seem to care about the crayfish. She only has eyes for the television, and is increasing the volume and playing with the colour knob so that the male news reporter's voice is louder, the colours brighter, like something drawn with school crayons. When the report's over, she seems to grow impatient. She starts to channel hop. Game shows. Adverts for Colgate toothpaste and Omo washing powder. Hop hop hop.

Hendrik fills each of the chests with ice. He must deliver these crayfish in time for the lunch-hour restaurant rush. He wouldn't mind eating something himself. With no breakfast in him, his stomach was an agony of gnawing hunger all the while on the boat. But he can't eat here. Not with that television nagging like a fishwife.

After making his deliveries and collecting his cash, Hendrik decides to head to the Red Sail. He hasn't been here for five years – but he's not sitting down for more than a few minutes before Sara comes out from the back. It's like she can smell him.

She whistles through her teeth, 'Look what the cat mos dragged in. I thought you'd emigrated to New Zealand.' She laughs her hacking cough. She's always smoked too much. When they were just children, getting up to mischief, it was Sara who started smoking first.

'I thought you work in the kitchen?'

'Pearl and Janni are off sick. So I'm on waitress duty today.'

'Can I order?'

'Menu coming, your royal highness. A beer in the meantimes?'

'No, brandy and Coke.'

'Whoohooo. Somebody's come into some money. But I've heard you been stealing everyone else's extra kreef business. One brandy and Coke coming – quicker than a Maserati.'

So Sara's heard. This morning, some of the other fishermen didn't greet him, and he thought something was up. Jaloesie. 'When good comes into your life, jealousy grows in the people's hearts faster than weeds. But when life is hard, then everyone is happy.' That's what his ma always used to say. Hendrik looks around. Everywhere on the restaurant's walls there are signs shouting rules. No bachelor parties! No split bills! No dogs! No shouting! No bathing costumes! No bare feet! Jissus, he doesn't remember this place being sommer so stuck up.

Sara comes back and plonks the glass in front of him. She takes out a pad and pencil from her back pocket and stands, cocking her body at a provocative angle, fluttering eyelashes that have too much blue mascara on them. On the tips there are blobs. Fok, she's his age. And what's with the bright red lipstick, and the red beret with the blue, red and white sparkling I LOVE PARIS on it? Has she gone and joined the EFF? He's even seen them in the village in their red berets. In his mind, Hendrik always calls them not the EFF but the EFT – ECONOMIC FOKKEN TRANSFER, because he knows their fat darkie chief only cares about lining his own pockets. Jirre, how can she go around advertising them? If he was her husband … only Sara never married.

'Calamari and chips, Monsieur?' From the smirk on Sara's face, he knows what she's thinking. Calamari and chips is her codeword for a soentjie and more, which they'd sometimes do, before Rebekkah.

Hendrik swallows and shakes his head. 'Ah nee, prawns and chips,' he whispers. In spite of himself, he can feel his piel stirring when she brushes against him to take back the menu. Jirre …

After his meal, Hendrik leaves enough money to cover the bill plus a fat tip, and flees. He decides to walk to the one-stop shop. He needs more airtime and an SMS bundle. He has plenty of calls and texts to return from customers wanting his lekker kreef. Maybe, now that he has more money, he should also think about getting a bigger chest freezer? If the money is good in the next few days, he'll go and put a deposit down on one.

When he's queuing to pay, his eyes fall on the newspapers in the rack. It's then that he sees it. The headline. DAM IT ALL, MR PRESIDENT! *President's daughter dams sacred river in Eastern Cape.* He picks it up and reads.

'The president has today been called to account by local villagers who claim that a development group owned by his daughter has diverted and dammed a sacred river estuary in order to build the family's holiday home. Spokesman for the Good for All Development Group claim that the new presidential homestead will be used to accommodate and entertain local and international dignitaries. The president explained that a golf course is necessary if the president is to host foreign dignitaries and officials, as many enjoy playing golf. However, locals claim that the river is a sacred place for their water people. In Xhosa culture, water people are thought to be ...'

In the accompanying large photo, Hendrik can see that the river beside the yellow diggers and crane is very low. Is it because of the drought, or because they've already drained and diverted it to make way for the spoilt president's latest toy?

CHAPTER FOURTEEN

'Oom, can we praat?'

'Ja, what is it Jarrad?'

His nephew hasn't stopped him in the street to talk for months.

'The women by the factory say you're the one who's stolen our orders with Ruben and Kobus. What's going on, man?'

Fokken skinnering … 'Ja, so what? It's no one else's business who I sell my crayfish to.'

Jarrad shakes his head. 'Pinkie and the factory have been supplying those restaurants for more than eight years. It's good advertising for us.'

What is his nephew talking about now? Doesn't he know Hendrik doesn't care about Pinkie's kak? All he wants to do is get home and show the visvrou – ruining his armchair with her puddles – this photograph on the front page of the newspaper. He wants to ask her, 'Is this it? Is this where you come from?'

She must have been really frightened, to have swum this far after they destroyed her home. All along the Eastern Cape coast, then around the southern tip, past Cape Town, then up the West Coast until she ended up here, exhausted and wounded. So she wasn't sent by Rebekkah? This water woman's Eastern Cape home place is too far from dams of the Karoo and Rebekkah's farm. So there's no message for him?

Jarrad's still talking, but Hendrik can't concentrate. There's that terrible ache in his heart. She's come here by chance? Nee, it is not possible. He *knows* Rebekkah sent her. His heart feels tight in his chest and he wants brandy. Lots of brandy. But Jarrad's still talking.

'Listen Oom, Pinkie is die moer in. If you don't stop stealing all our restaurant business, he won't let you sell your quota to the factory any more.'

'Tell Pinkie he and his factory can go and steek die fokken quota in hulle gatte op.' With that, Hendrik pushes past Jarrad and heads towards the liquor store. Brandy, he wants brandy.

'I'll pray for you!' Jarrad cries after Hendrik.

'Fok jou!' hisses Hendrik as he steps into the shop.

The Richards girl watches him suspiciously as he goes to the brandy section. Mooi Miss Klipdrift. One – no, two bottles. Lang tyd sonder 'n soen, my liefde. He pushes past the other customers, all locals buying their wyn cartons and beer, slams four blue hundred-rand notes on the counter and doesn't wait for his change. Let the Richards girl also shove it up her tight poes.

When Hendrik gets home, he immediately shows the visvrou the newspaper. There's a big photo of rolling green hills and a large river estuary running into the sea. And all around it, bright yellow tractors and diggers and other building equipment. While she's looking at the newspaper, clinging to it – yes, that's her place, he can see by her wide-eyed expression – he twists open a brandy bottle.

'They bring wealth and luck. But they are dangerous.' Xolani's words.

Dangerous ... Ha! What more does a drowning man like him have to lose?

When he's lekker drunk, he staggers to where she's watching the television. The newspaper is over the screen. The light flickers behind it. A skiet en donner, illuminating the image of the river, the not yet complete twenty-hole putt-putt course. A blerrie grap.

He knows better now than to turn the television off. He staggers back to slump down at the kitchen table. His eyes start to water as he talks, and it takes a few seconds for him to taste the salt and realise it's tears. He smears a sleeve across his face. He doesn't care about the tears and snot. He can't stop talking, and although the water woman isn't looking, hasn't even turned to take him in, he knows she's listening. He can feel it. He talks about Rebekkah. About the first day he saw her at the village Freedom Basaar.

About the time he took her to buy flowers. About the trip to the lighthouse, when she grew angry with him. And he talks about the day she disappeared. How he came home to find the dog locked in the bedroom and Rebekkah's handbag by the kettle. No note. No explanation.

'You and me, my friend,' he says, saluting the visvrou with the amber-coloured nectar, 'are a match made binne-innie *hel*. I've lost my wife to the sea, and you've lost your water home to a man.'

That night, when Hendrik finally falls asleep, he dreams that there's intruders in the house. In his dream, he can hear them tearing into all the cupboards and taking what's his, but he's frozen to the bed, stiff as a plank. In another room he can hear his mother, crying. Then Rebekkah. She's crying too. When he finally wakes up, just before 11 a.m., there are damp footsteps between his bedroom and the bathroom.

CHAPTER FIFTEEN

HENDRIK STOPS THE CAR. His head's still throbbing from last night's heavy drinking session, and when he burps, there's the faint taste of coffee and kots. Since he found the newspaper article about the President's new Transkei holiday house, he's lived on brandy like a fish in water. But today he's feeling a little better – he just put one dop in his coffee before heading into town. He rolls down the window for some air.

As he stood in Weskus Furnishers this morning, he worried he might be sick. But he managed to order the larger chest freezer, and fill in the forms for the monthly instalments, and get out again without throwing up all over their industrial grey carpet. He takes another gulp of fresh air. The sun on the ocean flashes like sparkling tin-foil. Hendrik stops the Toyota and gets out. There's a couple getting married on the beach. It's the start of January and another fokken year has started. Most of the local tourists will go home soon, but it's still a popular time for weddings. Chairs pushed into the sand and decorated with white satin slipcovers. Everyone's barefoot, except the pastor, who shifts in his leather shoes, his socks no doubt filling with sand and his neck and back damp with sweat. It is a hot summer's day. Die son brand weer die kak uit die aarde vandag. He can feel the sweat in his armpits, the beads dripping down his back.

Just then he sees it. A ripple of gold and black arrow markings as it slithers across the road and back into the shade and safety of the fynbos, silent and subtle as a cloud. A slang. Pofadder. Hendrik is always surprised at how fast they can move. Many people think they're bad creatures, looking to make evil, like in the Bible. But really they're mostly just minding their own business, until some idiot stands on them.

If Xolani is to be believed, then his visvrou could once have been that snake: 'They can be a snake, and then become a woman who's half fish, or just a woman – but she always leaves water wherever she goes. They come and start to act like your wife and bring you wealth. But they're very possessive, very jealous. They cannot share you with others.'

But he's never seen her as anything but a woman or a fish. Half fish, half woman, or just woman. And she's definitely not acting like a wife. He's the one still doing all the chores around the cottage. If anything, she just makes a mess, and it's up to him to keep the house in order.

'What if Rebekkah comes home and she finds this?' he complained to the visvrou the other day, after she'd left her crayfish shells in a heap on the kitchen table and sea-weed on the floor and chair.

The visvrou ignored him. Sometimes it's like having a teenager in the house. No talking or answering questions. Just taking, no giving ...

Only, she is giving. Excellent catches. That he cannot deny. But still, she's not matching Xolani's description of what this mamlamb ding should be. It makes no sense to Hendrik. All he *does* know is that just because she got kicked out of her estuary it *doesn't* mean that Rebekkah *didn't* send her. This is what he's decided, and it's a thought that feels like someone's thrown him a lifeline.

He's so grateful that this morning, even though he felt like kak, he decided he wanted to give the visvrou a gift – something special, what with all the money she's brought him these past ten weeks. After ordering the chest freezer, he walked the aisles of Pep and then Clicks, slurping from a can of Coke. But each time he picked up a fancy soap or rattled a bottle filled with candyfloss-pink bath salts like Rebekkah liked, he put it back. None of this, he knew, was right for the visvrou.

Hendrik starts the car again. On the seat next to him are the shells he's found. It took him a long time of search-ing the beaches on the reserve to find ones that weren't broken. He hopes she likes them.

Ja, after bumping into Jarrad and coming home with the newspaper, it's true, he made a bit of a fool of himself these past few days. The brandy hit him hard. Yesterday he even stopped at the Red Sail for a takeaway, and shouted and sang bawdy songs at the tourists while he waited: Jou ma se poes! Sy is 'n doos! Sy kom by my, sy klim my op …

Eventually Sara came out and sent him home with Daryll, who was there having a beer. Hendrik didn't fight, but let Daryll drive him home in his 4×4 and drop him outside his house.

'Just get into bed, boeta,' Daryll said.

Hendrik dismissed him with a wave of his hand.

Ja, he's not used to such strong stuff. Hendrik pulls into the road that leads to his cottage. Then he sees her, waiting outside. Kak! Sara! He should have known, after yesterday's scene. He parks and steps quickly out of the car.

'Môre, Hendrik, aren't you going to invite me in?' Sara asks, her arms folded. She's wearing a denim jacket with blue and purple rhinestones in the shape of a cowboy hat on each breast pocket, and an I ♡ Paris т-shirt. Hendrik sees she's also wearing a pair of pink slippers with black velvet ribbons. He knows it's because her feet are often sore from standing all day in the Red Sail kitchen.

'Dog kakked all over the floor and I haven't cleaned it yet,' he says. He must get Sara away from the cottage before she notices anything strange.

'Jissus, what's wrong with it?'

'Ate a … a rat.'

With Jakkals barking inside, he takes Sara by the arm and automatically leads her away from the cottage and down the road towards the beach. On the way down, they pass Rolf, who's driving up the hill in his car. Hendrik's brother-in-law greets Sara, but does not acknowledge him.

Sara arches an eyebrow as he passes. 'Everyone's afgepis that you're stealing their extra business. What's going on with you?'

At the beach, Sara flops to the ground and starts to unpack the bag she's brought. 'I had a feeling you wouldn't be asking me in. So I've brought coffee for us.' She opens the bag and pulls out a large thermos. But Hendrik won't sit. So everyone's been skinnering about him? Let them be pissed off. He doesn't care. He stands with his hands on his hips and looks down at Sara, who's kicked off her slippers and is twisting open the thermos.

'Just calm down and sit by me. I want to talk with you.' Without asking Hendrik if he wants any coffee, she pours him a steaming cup. It smells delicious and Hendrik wants to take the enamel mug, but he's not yet ready to accept Sara's offer of friendship.

'It's time for us to make peace, Hendrik. You need your friends. It's been long enough that you've been cutting yourself off from everyone.'

Peace? Friends? Hendrik longs for peace, and a part of him longs for the warmth of companionship, any companionship. But how can he have either when Rebekkah, the person he loves the most in the world, is still away and refusing to come home, and people like Sara spout lies about her being gone forever?

'It's Rebekkah who's sending me the extra kreef,' Hendrik blurts out.

'Rebekkah is not sending you the kreef, Hendrik—'

'You don't know everything. Rebekkah *could* be sending me the kreef.' He yells the last bit: 'And she's not dead, my wife is not dead!'

'Liewe Heiland, Hendrik! You're going mal, man. I never said Rebekkah is dead – but she's gone, and wherever she's gone to, she's not sending you the kreef!'

Well, at least Sara isn't saying Rebekkah is dood. That's something. Hendrik decides to calm down and sit next to her on the sand. He takes the mug she offers. The coffee's milky and sweet, just like Sara knows he likes it.

After a moment's silence he says, 'You've never been in love, Sara. You don't know what it's like. You can't just let go and forget.'

Sara blinks. 'I have a question, and just fokken answer it. If you knew something that might help someone you cared about but would also hurt them, would you tell …?'

Hendrik shrugs, 'Depends.'

'On what?'

'On if what you tell them will help them more in the end than if you don't tell them.'

CHAPTER SIXTEEN

THE LAST WEEK IN JANUARY. The tourists have finally gone, except for a handful of foreign stragglers. Every year it's the same. They arrive in clumps in mid-December, then in January they evaporate like the ocean mist when it's time to return to city schools and jobs. Once again, the village feels like home. Quiet. The houses near the shore are dark, their furniture covered with sheets, their ADT alarm beams on and blinking blue in the dark. It will stay like this until Easter, when many come again.

Hendrik isn't sure why all those extra alien bodies clogging up the village make him restless. He knows he likes their money when they buy his kreef. Maybe it's because they move in like an occupying army, marking everything as theirs, even his own oxygen.

Hendrik settles into his armchair and closes his eyes.

It's not entirely comfortable. The visvrou always leaves it wet, and these days Hendrik has to put a towel under him if he wants to sit in his own chair. She's asleep in the bath. Jakkals is sleeping too. So it's just him and Miss Klipdrift and his thoughts. Hendrik sips his drink. The colour is beautiful: that golden brown like when you sand wood, then varnish it, then polish it. And the taste. Ja, like nectar. Delicious. It warms the bloed and gives his mind the soft buzz he wants. Those expensive wines were all right. But they didn't calm his mind. That's what he wants. Hendrik takes another sip of brandy and thinks of the coffee and the slice of strange, uitlandse koek he had earlier with Sara. She baked it herself. Apple, only it didn't look like any appeltert Hendrik had ever seen before. Everything was upside down.

'It's French. They call it pomme ta-tin ...'

What is she going on about, Hendrik thought to himself, but he ate two slices because the koek, whatever it was, tasted buttery and delicious.

They've been meeting once a week, him and Sara. Not for long. But it feels good to speak about Rebekkah, even if only to hear her name said out loud by someone other than himself. Sara's a funny one. All these years of not talking – but just like that, he feels at home with her again. Maybe he'll meet her for a meal sometime, instead of just a quick coffee; but at some point she's going to have to apologise for how she disappeared when Rebekkah did, just when he needed her.

Genoeg! He wants to relax now and only remember

mooi things about Rebekkah. The things that make him love her, that make their relationship special. He watches the flames of the fire. Their dance does not have the water's rolling rhythm. If the ocean, even the stormy ocean, is like a juicy woman rolling her hips, then fire is like a woman's seductive tongue or beckoning finger. He can see Rebekkah's pretty, intelligent hands. So many times when he was courting her, he watched those hands and hoped and waited for them to grab his face and just pull him close for a deep soen.

Once, she said she was coming to visit and have dinner with him. He washed, he dressed in clean underwear with no holes in it and a nice-smelling shirt. He even brushed his teeth. Then he paced about the cottage and fussed about the food in foil he'd bought specially at the takeaway counter at Pick n Pay. Six o' clock, 6.30. He turned the oven off. He didn't want the chicken, rice and baked pumpkin to dry out. He checked the plates and knives and forks on the table again. The candle he'd put in the centre was burning down. He decided to blow it out and light it again when she arrived. He could almost taste her sweetness and the musty perfume between her legs. He tried to phone – once, twice, three times; sent four SMSes. But she never came.

At 9 p.m. he drove past her house. The lights were off. He stopped the car and climbed out. Should he knock? He didn't want to, but she'd said that she wanted to visit him. What had happened? In the end he decided to just go home.

The next morning, he got a text to say she was sorry. She'd fallen asleep after finishing her marking. Could they do it another day instead? Was he very upset? She hoped he didn't wait too long to eat.

But this is not the sort of story he wants to remember. Nee. He'll remember something else. Like the night it was raining. Hard and angry. Winter rain. The sort that fishermen like him fear because if you get caught out in it, it's sure to sink your bakkie boat and send you down to a briny death.

'To be honest, visvrou, that night didn't begin well either.' Hendrik can't help it. Even though he knows the water maiden's asleep, he needs to speak to her. He's found himself doing this more and more. Confiding things to her that he can't share with anyone else.

That night, the wind had picked up beyond the cottage windows and the clouds were low and thick, their grey bellies pregnant with rain. Soon, he knew, the ocean would be a battle of sea foam. Then the wind devils would swoop over the waters and into the village, like braks chasing their own tails, and rattle doors and windows.

Where does she go when she's not with me? That question was booming against the walls of his mind, like the waves banging against the rocks. Where, and who does she go with, when they weren't having one of their picnics or walks or whatever else he'd thought up as an excuse to see her? 'Because it was always me who was chasing her, visvrou, never the other way round.'

Where was she right at that moment? While he was in

this cottage, watching the fire, listening to the wind devils? The rain had started. It was falling fast and thick.

'Then there was a knock on the door. That's how I remember it.'

When Hendrik opened up, the wind rushed in and blew the folded newspaper open on the table. It was Rebekkah. She'd walked to him in the rain. Her white dress was wet through and he could see the outline of her bra. Her face looked swollen and her eyes red. Het sy gehuil? It was difficult to tell with the rainwater. Without a word, he let her in.

'Rebekkah became mine that night, visvrou.'

The rain, her coming to him in her white dress ... As if, like a towenaar, like Oom Daniel pulling a magical fifty cents from behind a kid's ear, he'd conjured her up purely through verskriklike verlange.

Hendrik gets up from the armchair and goes outside, stepping over the snoring dog. The visvrou, who he thought was sleeping, has come out of the bathroom and is now rummaging under the sink. There's the clank of metal buckets and plastic bottles. So she *was* listening to him. He continues to talk. Whether to the water maiden or himself, he doesn't know.

'One night, we fought a lot. About the tourists and my gemoan about them.' It started with that, but really it was something else that was pressing on Hendrik's chest. He'd just found out from Mrs Simons that it was Jarrad who was driving Rebekkah to the clinic for the monthly injection – 'My daughter, she saw your nephew with Rebekkah in town going to the clinic. Is everything all right with the family?' Fokken skinnerbek.

A part of Hendrik had hoped she'd changed her mind about having children. And then to hear that it was his nephew who was taking her, getting involved in their private matters ... Rebekkah didn't deny it when he confronted her. Did Jarrad know what they went for? 'I felt sick with jealousy, so I started an argument about the dog's fleas.'

But as soon as he did, he regretted it. Rebekkah was not a woman to back down: 'Maybe you'd prefer it if your sister came and cleaned. She doesn't seem to think I'm good enough for this family.'

Ja, Hendrik still can't forgive Lattie for not welcoming Rebekkah properly. And for what she said: 'There's something about her, Hendrik, that I don't like and I don't trust. It would be better for all of us if she went away.' Those words still burn him like bee-stings. Nee, something is wrong with that sister of his.

'And then she *did* disappear, visvrou. Just like Lattie wanted. But Rebekkah is not dead. Sara says so too. She is coming back. I know you also understand.'

Hendrik rubs his hands over his face. He can smell the drink, which is supposed to make him happy or at least forget. Then he hears the scrape of wood being dragged over concrete. Someone's moving the kitchen chairs. He looks up.

The visvrou is mopping, running the mop back and forth, back and forth over the concrete floor, as though she's trying to rub out a stain. Her face is pursed. Back and forth, back and forth. But she hasn't dipped the mop in water, so it isn't doing much.

On the wall of the bathroom are the newspaper pages with photos of what he thinks is her home, savaged by yellow diggers, fork trucks and cranes. Every time he goes to the one-stop shop, he looks to see if there are any more articles with fresh photos to give her. The paper is crinkled from being held so often, stroked by her damp hands.

It's morning, and Hendrik has been up and out on the boat, and come back with his crayfish. He's sitting at the kitchen table sorting through his latest orders with a pad and pencil. Twenty-four for here. Forty-five for there … thirty-two … Hendrik feels a tingle of anticipatory joy. All these bucks that will soon be flowing into his pockets. He knows he should probably start saving some, but he can't wait to go back to the liquor store to buy more delicious brandy. The Roberts girl has even started to greet, now that he's such a good customer. Ja, he wants brandy tonight. And vleis. Lamb. Lekker fat juicy chops …

A knock on the door. Jakkals springs up and starts barking. Someone's at the front door. Hendrik puts down the pencil and pad and freezes. Where is the visvrou? Doing something in the bathroom. Getting up as quietly as he can, taking care not to scrape the chair on the ground, he tiptoes to the window and looks through the curtain. Sara.

Two days ago she came, and he pleaded business

commitments and told her he'd contact her. He didn't. He meant to but it just slipped his mind. And now she's back, and this time he knows he won't shake her off so easily. He must put a stop to these spontaneous visits. It's one thing if they agree to go for a coffee, but he can't have her just showing up whenever she feels like it. She may see the visvrou.

'I know you're in there, Hendrik and I'm going no-where until you let me in!'

He steps out, taking care not to let Sara see too far in-side the cottage before he closes the door behind him. 'Sara, the coffee the other day was nice, and the apple tin koek ...'

'Pomme tarte tintin. It's *Frans*.'

'Um, ja, daai ding, but man, you can't just keep pitch-ing up—'

'Look, Hendrik,' she interrupts, 'I've been thinking about our talk yesterday and I've held my tongue long enough—'

Hendrik's cell phone rings.

'Hello, ja, Hendrik speaking. How many? Listen, I can't guarantee, Kobus. But if I can get them for you, I need three days and you'll have to pay in advance. Ja, sev-enty rands each. Ja, the price has gone up again. Because mine are the best.'

He hangs up the phone. 'What?'

'For fok sake, will you just listen to me, you stupid fool! I'm trying to tell you that I saw her.'

'Who?'

'Your Rebekkah.'

Hendrik's body goes cold. He steps towards Sara. 'When? Where?'

'With your nephew. Before she disappeared. Can we not talk inside?'

Hendrik shakes his head.

'All right, but the two of them were together, in his office by the factory. Hendrik. I'm sorry, but they were up to no good together.'

CHAPTER SEVENTEEN

'So i didn't do it. You know I wanted to, visvrou. Ja, my plan. Let myself into Jarrad's office using the extra keys in Rebekkah's handbag, the keys that Sara said she saw her use to open the back door to the factory. And I would bliksem him until he was fishpaste and then toss his body over the side of my boat and let the sharks feast on his fokken flesh. But I only got as far as taking him by the shirt: "You and my Rebekkah, did you fokken—"

'And he started snivelling. You'd think I'd cut his throat with my vlekking knife. He was begging, "Please uncle, I'm so sorry. But I loved her ..." and all this and that. He was pathetic, and I don't know, something came over me and my fist fell. Ja-nee, I told myself, you're not going to rot in a jail for him. So you're going to have to make another plan. He must suffer for what he's done.'

'Ja. He will pay. I've told him, I want that ding – you know, visvrou, that thing you darkies pay when one man foks another's wife? Nine thousand rands by tomorrow. He was too kak scared to do anything. Moffie poes. I should have asked for more. Ninety thousand. One hundred thousand. How much? I don't know. More. I'll make him … More and more until he must kak his broek, explaining it to his wife and Lattie and Pinkie. He must think of his own explanations for them. Ja, let him ask rich Pinkie for the money. I don't care. Let him rot in his lies. Ja, I didn't murder him. But the fokken little blerrie bastard poes piece of kak must pay.'

Valentine's Day and Sara and Hendrik are having a Kentucky Fried Chicken and chips picnic on the beach. Well, Sara is. Hendrik hasn't touched the food she brought him.

'Do I look like a man who wants to celebrate Valentine's Day?' he asked when she banged on his door at lunchtime with the bag of KFC.

'Who said anything about Valentine's Day? It's my day off. I thought we'd just have a picnic.'

Hendrik was still in his underpants and there was sleep crusted in his eyes. His mouth tasted like a rat had vomited in it. Sara smiled innocently and fluttered her eyelashes. She dangled the plastic bag on her index finger.

'I got Daryll to bring back Zingers and pieces. Chips too.'

The chicken smelt delicious and Hendrik felt his mouth start to water. He hadn't eaten a thing, only drunk for the past two days. His gut burned and churned from it.

'Vyf minute,' he told her, 'ek moet eers pis.'

Hendrik insisted they drive to a far-off beach where there was no one else around. He said that if he had to spend his day sitting with others, especially vryende teenagers or romantic Sunday strollers, he'd go and buy himself a gun and skiet and donner them all. The whole drive through town, Hendrik blasted the horn and shouted obscenities at any couple who were walking hand in hand. Sara just sat quietly.

Hendrik couldn't bring himself to speak with her at the moment. Whenever she opened her mouth, no matter what she said, all he heard were the words she'd used when she told him about his wife and Jarrad.

'It was early morning. I couldn't sleep. I was walking down to the beach. I saw her and something made me follow her. She didn't see me. But I saw her ...'

Sara said she saw Jarrad on his knees in front of Rebekkah, his face buried in her skirt. That she saw Rebekkah raking her fingers hard through his hair, and it looked like he was crying. Probably he was begging her to leave Hendrik, or she was begging him to leave Michel. Rebekkah had that cold, haughty expression she liked to wear. Ja, something fishy was up, Sara could tell. She has a nose for such things, she told Hendrik.

'So fok, Hendrik, it's time to leave off with your pining for that woman! You're killing yourself with all your wyn and moping.'

Hendrik sits scowling next to Sara. The ocean rolls and rolls before them and the seagulls swoop low, angling for a chip.

Sara lifts an eyebrow. 'Is nie my besigheid nie, Hendrik, but where did you get that new watch from?'

'Ja it fokken isn't. Late Christmas present.'

'And the car? Those are new rims and I see you've had it sprayed—

'So? Why should I drive a kak looking car?'

It's been a week since Hendrik's confrontation with Jarrad in his office. Since then, the klein fok has delivered his bucks like clockwork. First nine thousand, then another five. With that, Hendrik's gone all out. He's had the Toyota resprayed an angry, racing-car red and had new alloy rims put on it. He's also treated himself to this new watch, and a new leather jacket. But none of these expensive things makes him feel any better. In fact, with each envelope of money he only feels worse and worse, angrier and angrier. And Jarrad is supposed to pay another five at the end of the month.

'And that jacket?' Sara's arms are folded now. She's looking at him sternly.

'You ask too many questions. If you're going to be like this, I'm not going to spend time with you.' Hendrik unzips his knapsack and takes out a bottle of brandy. He carries a bottle with him everywhere now and is never without a good slop of it in his body. Without looking at Sara, Hendrik twists open the bottle and takes a greedy swig.

'Jirre, Hendrik ...' Sara puts down her chicken drumstick and picks up a chip. 'In France, these are called frites.'

'Not a fokken word, all right? I have things on my mind.'

Sara shut her mouth instantly. But Hendrik knows she won't be able to hold her tongue for long. Why did he agree to come with her? Liewe Vader. He can't remember ever feeling so angry before, not even after Anton was arrested and killed.

After ten minutes of silent munching, Sara leans over and takes Hendrik's chips. He pretends he doesn't notice. She tosses one to a gull that snatches it mid-air and flies off before the other birds can steal it.

'Très bon, seagull. In Frans that means very good. I'm learning French, you know, Hendrik. You never even ask.'

More silence. Hendrik can feel a question brewing in him now. A question he's been meaning to ask Sara for years. And now he feels angry enough to do it. Sara, after all, abandoned him too. It wasn't just Rebekkah. Sara looking down on his wife, telling him he'd been a fool, but her? What about the kak Sara's done to him too!

She's speaking again: 'You know, there's talk of a group of us going to stay by my sister in Cape Town for a few days. Villeen needs a holiday. It's been a hard year for her ... Maybe it would be good for you to come with us and get out—'

Before Sara can finish her sentence, Hendrik interrupts: 'Why did you disappear?'

'What? Me disappear? Where?'

'When Rebekkah left. You know I needed you then, and you just fokken disappeared, like her. Why? Was it some *man*?' he practically shouts, then takes another gulp of brandy. His head is soggy inside now, but his heart doesn't feel any calmer. The red fire of jealousy and anger still sears his blood.

For the first time, Sara looks genuinely shocked. 'You mean when I went to go stay by my sister's place in Cape Town for those seven months? You never asked anyone why? You don't know?'

'Know what?' Hendrik grabs a chicken drumstick from the box and tears into it with his teeth. There's chicken grease all over his chin. He wipes it with his sleeve. Before he can stop himself, a great belch escapes his lips.

Sara looks at Hendrik. Then, very quietly: 'Hendrik, you dom self-centred bastard. I had cancer in my breasts. I went for treatment by the Groot Schuur Hospital.'

CHAPTER EIGHTEEN

WHEN HENDRIK GETS HOME from the beach, the vis-vrou is unhappy. She's sitting silently, arms folded, waiting for him. As he enters he can feel her gaze, sharp with disapproval. Then Hendrik remembers. He forgot to feed her, and it's well after her usual lunchtime. He hasn't fed the dog either. They both watch him reproachfully as he kicks off his shoes and goes to the cupboard to get another bottle of brandy. He's left Sara on the beach. After she told him about her sickness, she stood up and began packing up her things to go home, saying she wanted to spend the rest of the day by herself. But Hendrik wasn't having any of it. No other woman was ever going to leave him again and make a fool of him, like some poephol.

'Nee, you are not going to fokken leave me alone here

on the beach! I will leave you!' He stumbled up and tripped over the picnic blanket, scattering sand into everything.

He shouldn't have driven, but he managed to get home. He pats his body … Where are the car keys? He pats his pockets. Still in the car. He may have left the car door open too. Fokkit. Let them steal everything from him. Everything he's ever loved. Let them steal this house too!

Hendrik refuses to look at the visvrou. He stumbles into the kitchen, bumping into a chair as he goes. There are some leftover chops in the fridge, but when he yanks open the door, he sees that the food inside is in disarray. The visvrou has been in here, looking for kreef. But those are locked in the new chest freezer, and only Hendrik has the key for that. Where are the lamb chops he cooked? Hendrik pulls at the food. Not here. Where? He turns and sees a few crunched bones by Jakkals's water bowl. She's fokken given them to the dog!

The visvrou is still watching him reprimandingly as he throws his new jacket over the back of the armchair.

'Don't you start now. How was I supposed to know she'd been sick? I thought she was just with some other man. Los doos Sara. You know she didn't get that by-naam for nothing … and Lattie could've told me.' But he knows that if she had, he probably wouldn't have heard. He was so deurmekaar about Rebekkah's disappearance during those months.

Los doos Sara … Hendrik opens another bottle of brandy. Only it's his Rebekkah who was the los doos in the end. His Rebekkah, who lived with him in this very house, sat in this very chair and ate with him at this very table; the woman he would've done anything for.

As if she can read his mind, the visvrou opens Rebekkah's lipstick and draws something on the kitchen table. It looks like a heart. Is it a heart? Is this dikgat visvrou mocking him?

He drinks from the bottle as he paces. Los doos los doos … The brandy dribbles down his chin and spills onto his jersey as he steps over the dog, who's still gnawing the last of a chop bone. She growls as he passes.

The room is now turning, as if the very house were a boat rolling on a stormy ocean. He just needs to sit down for a second. He slumps into the armchair. Papnat! She's been in his armchair again! And taken his chops to feed the brak!

Suddenly Hendrik is consumed with rage. He springs up and crashes towards the visvrou. 'You could show me some respect!' Hendrik jabs his finger at her. 'I am keeping you safe! Look how they hurt you at your place. They would hurt you again. There's probably no more river left. It is all a fokken fifty-hole putt-putt course and a fokken jacuzzi and who knows what else.'

The visvrou is still watching him. She is not smiling and she is not opening her mouth, but he can feel those yellow-green eyes. They have narrowed. She's sizing him up. Judging him. Angry. She's speaking to him with those eyes, but he will not listen. He squeezes his eyes shut, like he did that day when the news came about what had happened to Anton.

He is vrekmoeg of listening to people! They're worse than the seespoke and their jaaaaa jaaaaa jaaaaa gesukkel. Don't they know how much his heart is hurting? Doesn't this water woman know or care what it's like for him to know that, all along, his Rebekkah was betraying him?

Silently the visvrou gets up from the table and goes into the bathroom. Hendrik can hear the smooth splash as she sinks into the bathwater. He opens his eyes. Wait, he isn't finished talking with her yet! Another woman turning her back on him ... a fokken darkie vis woman! She can't just do whatever she likes in this house any more! It is him who wears the pants! They can't just ... can't just keep treating him like a kak straatbrak! The room is still turning and Hendrik is still as unsteady as a land rat on a boat for the very first time. But he doesn't care. He chases after her into the bathroom.

'Don't give me your troubles, visvrou. Hoor jy my? Ja, ever since you came here, my life has been kak! I feed you what you want, I take care of you. I don't make you clean or cook. All you have to do is be here so I can catch the kreef and make my money.'

In between angry sentences, he is swigging straight from the brandy bottle. Gulp gulp gulp. It's spilling down his chin. He's becoming angrier and angrier. He's not seeing her. Instead he is seeing Rebekkah and hearing Sara's words. The images are being carved again and again into his brain. Rebekkah and Jarrad on a beach blanket. Jarrad licking his wife's koek as they naai on his office desk, his chin and face shiny with her juices. Maybe they even did it in this cottage, in his own bed! Hendrik slams his palm against his forehead to stop the images.

Then he slams the brandy bottle onto the side of the bath. 'You are my *wife*! You are my wife and I should be able to do what I want with you!'

He's shouting at the visvrou. She is struggling. Rebekkah is struggling. Jakkals is snapping at him. He kicks the dog and hears it yelp in surprise and pain.

'You are my wife! You are mine you are mine you are *mine!*'

He jumps into the bath and pulls her up with one hand, while trying to pull down his trousers with the other. He hasn't touched her since that day he wrapped her up and brought her home. She's freezing, but he doesn't care. There is the fire of Lucifer burning in him now, and he will not stop until he gets what he wants, what he is owed.

Rebekkah, I want a baby with you.

He's out of the bath now, soaking, fighting to get her out too. Rebekkah is the visvrou, thrashing and fighting. Hendrik starts to drag her towards the bedroom. Jakkals is barking, gnashing at him, but he gives the dog another mighty kick. Rebekkah is sinking her nails into his flesh, drawing blood. They are the visvrou's nails, but Hendrik sees only his wife. He picks her up and puts her over his shoulder like a sheep's carcass, like a sack of potatoes, and carries her into the bedroom. Dumps her on the bed and grasps her arms to keep her fast as he tries to unbutton his

jeans. Then, for the fourth time since her arrival, the water woman lets out a tooth-shattering roar.

Sara is still awake when Hendrik finally reaches her cottage. It must be after 3 a.m. All the other house lights
have long gone off and the villagers are sleeping soundly,
Hendrik is sure, unaware of his torment and pain. He
thinks his foot has stopped bleeding, although it's difficult
to tell in the dark. He stands under a streetlight and tries
to roll up the leg of his jeans and push down his sock, but
the pain makes him yelp and he gives up.

After the visvrou's scream, he slipped and cut his heel
pretty badly on a piece of broken glass from his shattered
brandy bottle. The cut still stings like hell, and the ankle's
pretty swollen and painful to walk on. Hendrik limps up
to Sara's door and knocks.

She answers wearing an apron. She must be baking
one of her Franse koek concoctions where everything is
upside down, Hendrik thinks. In the background a voice
is reciting words: '*Oooo eh laaaa gare?*' Sara frowns. Her
eyes pass down to his foot and the blood on his jeans.
Without a word, she steps aside to let him pass.

The rage has left him now. The water woman's furious
scream burst it like a lanced boil. He's spent the last four
hours walking the beach with his bloody swollen ankle,
until he grew so cold in the pitch dark that he couldn't go
on any more. Intermittently, the memory of what he tried
to do to her filled him with such self-revulsion that he
threw up his drink onto the sand until there was nothing

left in his stomach but bile. His head is not yet clear, but his blood must be running stone-cold sober.

Inside Sara's cottage, Hendrik can smell pastry cooking in her oven. Then he sees the posters. On the wall next to the kitchen table, there's one of that famous building, the Eiffel Tower. Others of lovely scenic canals with green banks and mud-coloured water. The cottage feels warm and bright, and all Hendrik wants to do is flop down and have Sara take care of him. But she doesn't move from the entrance.

'All right,' she says, 'what do you want? I'm lekker busy, you know.'

'I didn't know you like art,' Hendrik says feebly, pointing at a poster of that painting of a long-haired, smiling woman. Hendrik knows that one, it's very famous, he just can't remember its name.

Sara shrugs. 'It seems there's plenty you don't know about me. What did you do to your foot?'

'Slipped. It's nothing.' Hendrik tries, but he can't keep the note of self-pity from his voice. 'Do you have a Panado?'

While Sara goes to find a Panado and some proper bandages – 'Because you're fokken spreading bloed through my house. Everyone's going to think I committed a murder—' Hendrik leans back in the armchair she's told him to sit in. 'Put your foot up. If you've sprained it, it shouldn't be on the ground.' He does as she commands. He will not fight her any more. He needs help.

'What are you listening to?'

Still nothing from Sara. The CD continues: 'Je m'appelle. Michelle and Jean meet for a coffee in a cafe. Jean tells Michelle he is eighteen and likes football.' He knows he's hurt her feelings one too many times, and his ignorance about her past illness is sleg. He wants to make it right, but he doesn't have the strength tonight. The truth is that he's come to her so that she can take care of him.

'Do you think Lattie knew too? That's why she wanted Rebekkah to go ...' A thought occurs to him: 'And that's why she wanted those keys so badly when the police came to the house? She didn't want anyone to find out Rebekkah had keys to Jarrad's office. Then they would've asked all sorts of questions.' This will win him more sympathy from Sara – if she knows just how many people have betrayed him.

Sara turns to looks at him, wiping her hands on a lappie. With a sigh, she pushes the button to stop the CD.

'I'm sorry, Hendrik. People are very disappointing.'

'Listen. I'm sorry too. I didn't know that you'd been sick. No one told me, and it was a bad time. Rebekkah, you know, it was when she disappeared and I only thought of that.'

'Jirre, but you've always been a bit of a self-centred kont.' Hendrik watches as she puts down a basin of warm water with some Dettol in it. He can smell its sharp medicinal smell. Sara goes on: 'Always worrying about your own problems and hurts first. I remember when Anton was going to varsity. Jissus, you gave him a hard time. And then, remember how you went around telling people that he wasn't really at varsity? That he was in trouble and had run away from home? Just because you didn't like that he'd gone ... so you made up your own story.'

As she scolds him, Sara bathes his wound. Hendrik clears his throat uncomfortably. He is lucky to still have her in his life. Because what she is saying is true. Yes, he did remember telling people that. But Sara wasn't finished with him yet. It was like a wave that'd been gathering in her for years now finally had a chance to thunder down on Hendrik, and she wasn't going to stop until he was thoroughly drenched.

'Ja, you really, you can't even see past your own fokken piel! And when you do talk, it's only ever about your own fokken self. Never ask about the other person. You're not the only fokken one whose heart is sore. This whole fokken village and this whole fokken country is full of fokken hartseer people haunted by their ghosts, Hendrik. You talk all the time about your seespoke. But there are also sickness ghosts and dead-children ghosts and missed-opportunity ghosts, and lost-love ghosts.'

She rubs his foot dry with a towel. The wound is clean now. She unpacks some bandages from an old shoebox.

'You are right, Sara.'

'And listen, I'm not saying what your nephew and Rebekkah did was right, and I know this is difficult for you to hear, but I think they might have married if it wasn't for Lattie and Pinkie Booyens. You know what they can be like. They should have just sommer married each other, I hear they were secret varsity sweethearts. But Jarrad was already promised to Michel and, you know, all that money. You didn't see your nephew at the memorial. Neither did I. I was already having treatment down by the hospital in Cape Town. But I heard it was snot and trane all over the place, and Michel refused to stay for the speeches.' As she speaks, she wraps the bandage around his foot. 'That doesn't mean Rebekkah didn't love you too, but it was complicated. The heart is complicated and it can sometimes do stupid things when it's hurt or confused. You're not the only one trying to sail his boat on a stone sea.'

With a firm but tender gesture, Sara ties the bandage on the side of his foot. 'Voi-là! That should hold it, but you maybe should go to the clinic tomorrow.'

Hendrik gulps. All he can do is nod. He can feel one, then two, then more tears start to fall. He grits his teeth. He doesn't want to cry in front of Sara. Ek is 'n man, not a stupid little boy being bliksemed by his pa.

Sara's tone softens. 'You look like last year's kak. Why don't you go and sleep? I'll finish what I'm doing here.'

Hendrik falls asleep in Sara's bed. The sheets stink of talcum powder. But, for the first night in five years, he doesn't dream of Rebekkah. Instead he dreams that a great flock of seagulls land on Sara's cottage roof. When they open their beaks, he grits his teeth, expecting the usual screech and complaining caw-caw. But that doesn't come. Instead the gulls sing bubbles of sound, popping, green, purple, pink, violet. And their kak isn't normal birdshit either, but blobs of paint.

When Hendrik wakes up, he finds Sara asleep in her armchair. One foot is sticking out of the knitted blanket. The varnish on the toenails is red, white and blue. He doesn't want to go home yet and face the visvrou. But he can't stay here. He must go back. He pulls the blanket over Sara's foot and creeps out.

CHAPTER NINETEEN

'c-h-o-u-f-l-e-u-r? That's not a word.'

'Dis 'n Franse woord.'

'You can't use another French word.' He's already let her use fleur, the French word for flower, she told him. And now this.

'Why? We're playing Afrikaans Scrabble with an English Scrabble set. I think we should be able to use any language if it's in our bloed.'

'Jy is nie 'n fokken Hugenoot coloured nie! Jy's net 'n coloured, 'n Gam. You shouldn't be ashamed.'

'Who said anything about being ashamed? Jissus, you can talk a klomp kak, Hendrik.'

Hendrik and Sara have been up talking and drinking coffee and playing Scrabble most of the night, and now it's almost dawn. Hendrik doesn't mind. He and Jakkals have been staying by Sara's place for more than a week now, while he tries to dry out, and this argument has become a regular ritual for them. Sometimes it goes on right through the night until the orange light spills through the window onto the kitchen table and Sara's little collection of ornaments that she keeps in the glass-fronted cupboard opposite the sofa where they sit.

Without the drink, Hendrik can't sleep, and he's asked Sara to help him. It's been a long time since he last asked someone for help, but he knows he can't do it without her. He goes home three times a day to check on the vis-vrou and to make sure she has enough food. Whenever he's by the cottage, he feels her watching him, staring. She doesn't approach him, but he can feel her eyes. And he still can't look at her. Why doesn't she just leave, he often wonders. If she hates him so much now? But the crayfish is always eaten and she seems to be keeping herself busy, although what with, Hendrik isn't sure. She no longer flips through the radio or television channels when he's there.

'Your ma was a boorling with Boesman bloed – so you can use a Boesman word if you want,' Sara continues. She stubs her cigarette out in a leftover slice of quiche. She says it's too salty, but Hendrik thinks it's one of her better French concoctions. He's eaten two slices himself.

I don't know any Boesman taal, Hendrik thinks to himself as he squints at the collection of letters on his small green Scrabble stand. They're waiting for him to give them order, but Hendrik can't think of any word, in any language, which uses two Rs, a z, an s, a G and a T. His eyes scan the board again, looking for somewhere, anywhere to use his s. That's a good trick of Sara's, to just make something a plural. But the board is chockers and there are no easy points to be had.

Hendrik bites his bottom lip as he concentrates. Sara and her fokken stories. Next she'll be saying she's the Queen of Sheba. But she's right about his ma being a boorling. Her family was born and bred in the village for generations, but it was said that originally her people were those who lived in the beach caves, long before anyone else set foot here. That's how come she could tell you what plant was good for eating, or how renosterbos was good for the maagwerkings in children and douwurmbos could fix ringworm. Her ouma had taught her, and her ouma before her. No one knew where the knowledge originally came from, everyone just knew it, and knew it had been passed down.

'And you know, your Auntie K was always saying your people married with Xhosa peoples, long ago, so you can use Xhosa words too. I won't mind. We're all mixed mense in this country. That's what your Auntie K always said.'

Sara has lit another cigarette and is totting up the points so far. 'Chou-fleur, sixteen plus double word score, makes thirty-two. That gives me ninety-two so far and you, seventy-eight. You'd better stretch your brain a little more, my friend. Pen-se, as the French say.'

It was no use trying to talk sense into her. If Sara

wanted to have Hugenoot-bloed like those rich whites up Franschhoek way, then so be it. Let Sara believe what she wants to believe.

'So jy leer Frans … to go where in France?'

'Paris! First I'm going to go there on holiday, and if I like it, I'm going to try and find work in a restaurant kitchen. That's why I must keep practising making their sort of foods. No one wants snoek frikkadels or malva pudding in France.'

Hendrik knows the story by now, he's heard it many times since coming to stay; but he knows Sara enjoys telling it, so he keeps asking, and acts like it's sommer the first time he's hearing it.

'It was Jane, my friend, who gave me this Scrabble board, who made me think. You should go and do your dreams. Just go and live, woman!'

Hendrik nods. Jane was Sara's whitey friend who played Scrabble with her while they waited for their turns on the chemo machines. Only Jane hadn't made it, like Sara did. Her breast cancer was too advanced and too aggressive.

'Green, black or pink, everyone dies sooner or later. Rich or poor. Afrikaans or Engels. Death does not mos discriminate. That's one thing I learnt by that hospital. Jane was Engels en fit and she didn't make it. But I made it. I went to her funeral. It was hard. I was still sick. I'd lost my hair. But I went.

'Then I remembered what my pa and ouma always said about us having French bloed, and how that was why we all had very light skin, and our hair was never sommer *coarse* …We had Hugenoot in our bloed, from when our people still worked on the farms. That was when I began to make my plan.'

Hendrik leans back in the armchair. The letters are defeating him, but he must concentrate. Otherwise his longing for the wyn gets so bad he can hardly breathe. It's like a fist gripping and squeezing him. The first few days were the worst. All he could think of was the wine. Wanting it. Missing it. It was worse than the longing for a lover. Worse even than missing Rebekkah. His whole body cried out for it. But spending time with Sara has helped. Without her, he wouldn't have gotten through the past week without giving in to the longing. He doesn't even dare spend too long alone at home, in case his willpower fails him.

'What about travel? Don't you think you want to see some of the rest of this world?'

Hendrik looks up. Sara's watching him carefully. It's almost like she can sense when he's struggling.

Why? What could the world and foreign countries have to teach him? But there's something else. Another thought that he's been having since the incident that night with the visvrou. A plan that's been brewing.

Hendrik puts a 'G' and a 'T' down and sits back. 'G-A-T.'

'*Gat*, Hendrik? Is that your best—?'

'I've been taking money from Jarrad.'

'What?' Sara puts down her pencil.

'Making him pay me lobola every week.' Hendrik puts

his hand into the letters bag and pulls out three beige letter tiles. He can't look Sara in the eye, but he imagines her expression.

'What? Lobola is what the blacks pay to *get* a wife, not if they cheat with another man's wife—'

'Ja, well, I want to do something with that money.'

There's a long pause from Sara. 'How much has he given you?'

'Almost twenty thousand. It's been more than a month.'

'Fok ... You must give it back.'

'Nee. I've told him he must pay. It's guilt money. I'm going to buy a boat with it. A bigger boat that can travel overnight.'

'Why?'

'I want to make a journey.'

Those first days of going dry, whenever he was by his own cottage, he'd open all the cupboards where he used to keep his wyn. He knew it was gone. He'd got rid of it all quickly, before he lost his nerve, the day after the incident with the visvrou. But he couldn't help it: he opened those cupboards anyway, relieved that there was none there, but still a part of him hoping that he'd missed a bottle or box. When you're going without the wyn, the first few days are very bad, it's true.

But the worst, he's fast learning, is after a week, then two, when you realise you can never ever taste it again. Not even one tiny dop, because if you do, that will be you, overs. The wyn will have you in its grip forever and drag you down down down until you're as good as a drowned man. That's what Hendrik confessed to Sara one night as they lay in bed together – not naked, fully clothed, but holding each other.

They haven't had sex. They haven't even kissed. But each night, when they finally get to bed after the Scrabble, they lie side by side and Hendrik cries. He cries and cries and cries. More than he ever cried when Anton died, or his parents, or even when Rebekkah disappeared. A part of him is ashamed. That he's mourning and grieving losing the wyn more than he thinks he's ever grieved for anything else in his life. He can't help it. It's been his friend, his one true friend all these years, ever since Rebekkah went. But also not a friend. Or the sort of friend who comes by your place and empties your cupboards and borrows your wages but never pays you back.

Hendrik sits down at the kitchen table. He hasn't tidied properly in weeks and all around him, the kitchen is in chaos. Rebekkah wouldn't like this. But it doesn't matter what she thinks any more. She isn't coming back. Ja ja ja, he hears the seespoke sigh. Never never never.

A shudder shakes his body. He must keep going. Although at the moment he's not sure what for. He bends down and opens the icebox at his feet. Five crayfish to defrost. That's what he leaves for the visvrou, three times a day. He gives her the biggest kreef he has – it's the least he can do, after the other night. Hendrik shudders again. He doesn't want to think about that. He hasn't been able to bring himself to give them to her personally, or to speak to her. He just leaves them on the kitchen table and goes back to Sara's place, or out on the bakkie boat, or to make deliveries. When he gets back, the plate always just has the shells on it, so he knows she's still eating at least. Should he go and fetch more fresh seawater? He'll do that later, and leave the buckets outside the bathroom for her to pour the water into the bath herself. He hasn't set foot in the bathroom since that night. He barely sets foot in the house, except to feed her and check she's okay. Ja, he thinks this visvrou must hate him.

But this morning he has some important news for her, news which he hopes will begin to change things for the better. When he's finished laying out the crayfish, he goes to the bathroom door. He doesn't cross the threshold. This is her private space now. But he stands in the doorway and speaks into the darkness.

'I'm sorry, visvrou. Are you awake? Can you hear me? I'm saying I am sorry. I was drunk and I was, you know, very angry. But I'm not making excuses. Please, visvrou, just listen, I want to tell you something. I'm going to take you home. You see that photo on the wall, of your place? I'm going to help you go back there. I'm going to help you get it back. Ikhaya, vis maiden. I'm going to take you home.'

CHAPTER TWENTY

DARYLL SAYS HE HAS A COUSIN of a cousin in Saldan-
ha with a wooden boat to sell. Hendrik knows there are
plenty of fibreglass boats out there for a reasonable price,
but he wants a wooden one. A real visserman's vessel. He
knows wood, how a wooden vessel behaves in the water.
When he was a boy, his pa took him with to Pete's workshop sometimes so that he might learn a thing or two. In
the school holidays, he was allowed to help with sanding
and recorking, and even varnishing and painting.

Naturally, his pa watched him like a hawk, but he also
taught him some useful tricks. Like how you should box
half the brush up with duct tape, to keep the bristles nice
and firm and to stop the varnish from dribbling down the
handle and making a mess.

The boat that cousin Marlon has for Hendrik is a

twenty-four-foot ex-fishing vessel, with a blue and red
hull, a tiny wheelhouse and a small cabin. The hull, he
says, knocking the wood with his hand, is solid. And
tarred. But the deck, the cabin, the heads – those all need
some TLC. She was seized by the coastguard, Marlon says,
in a raid on abalone poachers. He shows Hendrik the cer-
tificate of compliance that proves she's seaworthy.

Hendrik wonders how a boat seized by the coastguard
for illegal perlemoen fishing has come to be in Marlon's
yard. But he's getting it for a good price, so he won't ask
too many questions.

Hendrik looks up at the keel. No sign of cracking or
repairs. That's good. He raps on the hull with his knuckles. It's important that the hull is solid, although he's sure
he'll have to repair and replug some of the corking between the boards. Sorting this out takes a long time, and
he feels like he doesn't have much of that. He wants to get
the water woman home before winter and the seas grow
too rough for him to make the journey with her.

Is it really almost five months since he found her on
the rocks at the reserve? He can't believe it.

'And the engine? Any water in it?'

Marlon scratches his head under his cap. 'Honda.
Looks all right. Starts.' Marlon takes out the dip stick. It
looks clean. Hendrik knows what to look for: foamy and
muddy like a chocolate milkshake means water in the engine, and you don't want that. But you never know with
engines until you start them up in the water.

'How far do you want to go with her?'

'Eastern Cape. Transkei.'

The boat man sucks his teeth and licks his lips. 'Ja-nee. She'll need some care first, but I think she can make it.'

As part of the deal, Marlon is lending Hendrik the boat scaffolds so that he can do the repairs himself. He is parking it in the yard in front of his own house, and has moved his Toyota up the street.

After the delivery, he circles the boat and introduces himself to her properly. It's a two-way relationship when it comes to boats and men who skipper them. You show her respect and take care of her, and there's a good chance she'll take care of you too. It's a bit like it must've been in the old days, when men rode horses. The horse became more important to some men than their wives and families. And Hendrik certainly knows a few fishermen who'd ditch their wives and marry their bakkies, if they could.

Your boat doesn't give you a dik bek. It helps you put bread on the table, and when you're on it, you are your own master. No bowing and scraping to some boss who doesn't give five cents for you, and would happily trade you for one of the nakkas if he'd work for less. It's always been a great source of pride for the Coloured families of this village that they have their own boats, even if they're smaller than this one. This one is a real boat. An overnight boat. And its arrival immediately stirs curiosity and questions in the village

'What you want a new boat for? You get extra quotas?' Daryll asked him suspiciously. The other fishermen crowded round too.

'Nee man, she isn't going to be used for fishing. Don't worry. I have other plans for her.'

Hendrik doesn't tell the men what plans, but they seem satisfied that he won't be stealing any more of their business. Anyway, Hendrik knows that rumours are already circulating, thanks to Jarrad, that this boat is to be used for overnighting and kerk business.

Kerk business fok. But Hendrik doesn't want trouble. He just wants to be left to fix her up as quickly as he can and make her fit for the voyage. When Hendrik sets sail, he plans to take almost nothing. Some clothes. The dog – he can't abandon her after all this time. But the rest ... he wants to be free. To cut his ties and begin again. But first he must take the visvrou home.

He knows how to fix a boat. He knows. He must get wood. He must get the correct tools. A hand saw. Nails. Vices. Grips. He wishes Pete was still alive, with his old workshop. Now if there's a problem with the bakkies, the men do it themselves to save on costs. But they don't know about proper boats, a boat like *Amanda*. Hendrik walks around her, looking at her keel. Now that is a lekker keel. Attached to the boat, not just lumped on the back so it can break off at the slightest bit of sea trouble. A rock, a hidden sand bank. Both can do serious damage to a loose keel.

Hendrik turns – a group of teenagers has come to snoop. Bloody one-donkey town. You can't fart here, he thinks, without everyone knowing you're going to take a kak.

'Building a coffin, Oom?' the boys ask, laughing.

Hendrik thinks that one of them is Jerome's daughter's boy. He wants to take their insolent heads and bang them into the wall. Hotnot poes. But he slows his breathing and tries to smile. 'No, a proper boat to go on an adventure.'

Now they look interested. 'Where you going to go, Oom? Europe? America?'

'In a boat this big? Are you dof? Along our coast, all the way to the Transkei.'

The boys look bored again. 'Why do you want to do that, Oom?'

'To help ...' He pauses. How can he describe his relationship with the water maiden? 'To help a friend.'

The boys leave, the faces glued again to their cell phones, playing their pop music. Hendrik sighs. Those barnacles are calling him. He picks up the scraper. Time to get to work.

Sara has come to see the boat and she's brought Xolani. Hendrik's happy to see him – it's been almost a month – but when they arrive, Sara asks to go inside to get a glass of water, and he must make one of his excuses so that she doesn't discover the visvrou, who's once again sitting in the bath with the lights off. Earlier, she was snoozing in front of the weather forecast. When Hendrik passed her, her eyes snapped open and he could feel her watching him, could sense a flash of her small teeth.

'How come you never invite me into your place?' Sara asks, her arms folded.

Hendrik quickly changes the subject: 'Xolani, did you go away to the Eastern Cape?'

'I stayed here, Hendrik.'

'But why, I thought you darki ... you people always go home to the Eastern Cape for Christmas time?'

'This is my only home now,' Xolani replies, not looking at Hendrik but staring hard at the boat's propeller.

Sara gives Hendrik a look like, nee, ask no more of your questions. And Hendrik can't think why, but he decides not to push any more. Anyway, the important thing is that she's no longer asking to go inside. He pours coffee from his flask and passes the mug around.

'These blades will need to be fixed,' Xolani says after he's had a sip.

'Um, ja. Rust. Do you know about boats?'

Xolani nods.

Hendrik is surprised.

'Xolani worked in the docks by Port Elizabeth. When I told him you'd bought a boat, he said he'd come and take a look at her.'

Once again, it seems Sara knows more about people in the village than Hendrik does. Although that's no surprise. For the past few years, it's true, Hendrik has lived with his head up his own backside. There could have been a world revolution, or a meterorite could've struck Johannesburg, and he probably wouldn't have cared or noticed.

Ja, *Amanda* is a fine boat, but a neglected one. Hendrik pats the bow. The boards need recorking – but just the ones on the starboard side. 'Three days of scraping at her, and now the barnacles are off I can start the sanding,' he tells Sara and Xolani. 'But it's still going to take me weeks and weeks to get everything done.'

Hendrik starts unrolling an extension lead for the sander. But Sara says she's brought lunch and convinces him to stop first and eat: 'Nothing worse than sawdust in your frites …' Sitting on tins of varnish and paint, the three of them tuck in. Sara tosses Hendrik a packet of chilli sauce. 'Compliments of the Red Sail.'

All around the village, she tells him, people are skinnering about Hendrik's new boat. Jarrad, she tells Hendrik, has told the Pastor and Pinkie that his uncle is on some sort of holy mission. 'He says you're preparing a Noah's ark. A small Noah's ark … but everything's smaller nowadays, like cell phones and laptops. So why not the ark too? And Noah, he was a righteous man, but he was not perfect, just like you. It's our duty to support you.'

'But I'm not taking any animals …'

'He says you're taking the Gospel. The Word of God. He's telling people you've stopped drinking and have found Salvation, and you want to travel in your boat to help and save others. And then that Richards girl jumped in – "Ja, it's true. He hasn't been to buy by my shop for weeks!"'

Xolani smiles but says nothing.

Apparently, Jarrad had sweated as he spun his story for the pastor and the congregants to justify the money he had given his uncle. Sara reports this all to Hendrik.

'Ja, but I've given him a way out. I'm selling the old

cottage to him and Pinkie. So he can just say that the money is part of what he is paying me for that.'

At this revelation, there's silence from Sara and Xolani. Both look at him with expressions of disbelief. Hendrik nods. He'd like to spend more time talking with them, but he's given himself just seven weeks to get the boat ready to sail. After years of sitting on his backside moping about Rebekkah, it actually feels good to work this hard at a proper project. But he'll have to spend every hour he can, he tells them, day and night, doing the necessary work.

His sense of urgency is also fed by something else. The truth is, he thinks the visvrou is in trouble. She's not been the same since the night he dragged her out of the bath. She's not eating much: often, these days, the crayfish are only picked at or half eaten, never devoured. The cottage is starting to smell of old seafood, like it did before he figured out that she liked kreef. This morning, when he was by the house, she came into the kitchen wearing Rebekkah's yellow dress, a cardigan, a jacket and, for the first time, socks. She seemed cold, but how can a fish, which is cold-blooded, get cold? Hendrik worries that with all this time spent on land, living on legs instead of swimming in the sea, she's forgetting what it means to be of the ocean. But she isn't happy in her human skin either. Her complexion is grey and her flesh seems to be itchy and flaking.

And then there's what she's doing by the house. Often when he goes there, he finds that the cupboards have been emptied. All the salt and the porridge and the coffee poured out of his canisters. She's looking for something. She is longing. He knows what longing looks like. He knows the signs, clearer than the Southern Cross. Even the photographs of her home cut out of the newspapers don't seem to help any more.

He wants to tell her, moenie worry nie. He wants to touch her, but he doesn't dare. Apart from when he lifted her into his boat and carried her into the house and lowered her into the bath, and that horrible incident when he tried to drag her to the bed, he's never touched her. The best thing he can do for her, he knows, is to get her home. Take her back to her place and to those like her. She doesn't belong here. He'd like to keep her, but she doesn't belong. And the sooner he can do it, the better for her and maybe the better for him, although he knows he won't find it easy to be without her. Another loss. Another sort of death. Someone falling out of his life just as he's gotten used to them and started to care.

Last night in Sara's bed, Hendrik felt like he could hear the visvrou calling for home, under the door, across the concrete. Though not with her terrible shriek. With something else. He didn't want her to go, didn't want to let her go, *don't go stay with me don't go stay with me don't go stay with me* ... he rolled over and put the pillow over his head. As he fell asleep, it was with the image of all the ants, cockroaches and spiders in the house scuttling towards her, answering the visvrou's call for home.

Then he dreamt of Rebekkah. She'd walked into the house, feet covered in sand. In the dream, Hendrik walked out of the bedroom and saw puddles of water leading from the bathroom to the front door. It was open. He rushed to the bathroom. The bath was empty. The visvrou has gotten out, he thought in a panic. He forgot to lock the door last night and she'd gotten out. He grabbed his keys off the kitchen table and ran outside to the car.

But he didn't find the visvrou outside. Instead he found Rebekkah. Her clothes were wet. She was covered in dark, slimy seaweed. 'You must leave me alone now, Rebekkah. I don't want you to visit me any more!' he cried out in the dream. 'I've lost the water woman!'

He woke up crying.

Hendrik coughs. He wants a drink, but instead reaches into his pocket and pulls out a packet of cigarettes. He offers one to Sara and one to Xolani. For a few minutes, they all sit smoking in silence.

Then Xolani stands up. 'I must go and do some repairs at the school. Skollies have been coming and stealing brass. There's a leak now in the toilets. But I will come back afterwards to help you.'

'To help me?'

Xolani nods. 'Yes. If you want to have this boat ready before next Christmas, you will need more hands than just yours. I will help you after 3 p.m. today and tomorrow again after church.'

Later in the afternoon, it's not so hot and Hendrik walks to the cemetery, his long shadow following him. He walks among the stones, careful not to step on new graves. For the first time, he stops now and then to read the names and inscriptions.

He pulls out weeds from all three graves, Anton's and Ma's and Pa's, and picks up three beer bottles and some entjies. He doesn't know when last he tended their graves. But he plans to come back every week until he and the visvrou leave on their journey.

'Okay, Anton, so I'm going to take her home. I just need more time.'

You know where I come from used to be an ocean too. Rebekkah. Memory. He doesn't want to. He wants her to go now. Go for good. *It is all stone now and koppies but once water used to flow there. My ouma, she showed me stones. Stones with fossilised fish trapped in them.* Ja, Rebekkah, ja. I am taking her home. Just leave me the fok alone, okay?

CHAPTER TWENTY-ONE

HOUR AFTER HOUR, day after day, it seems to Hendrik that he does little more than eat, sleep, sand, mend, plug, scrub and varnish. Xolani comes whenever he can. Together they open giant tins of wood varnish and paint with screwdrivers. Empty turps bottles now fill his dust-bin like the wine bottles and boxes did before. It's good. All this hard labour helps Hendrik to keep his mind off his body's longing for the liquor. How it calls and calls him to it, like hands waiting to pull him down under the waters. He will not give in. He's told himself he'll only work harder on the boat if the cravings get worse. But he's smoking again. Sometimes as many as twenty a day. It helps.

Hendrik smoothes the splintered and uneven boat boards with an electric sander, the sander's extension lead running all the way back to the house and through the window. He drinks strong black coffee, or sometimes coffee sweetened and lightened with condensed milk. Sometimes he and Xolani talk while working on the boat, and sometimes they say nothing for hours. Just get on with their various tasks. Getting *Amanda* seaworthy as quickly as possible. That's all that matters now. In the evenings, when he's too tired to work any more, he goes to visit Sara.

He's putting on weight from their time together. He shows the visvrou his stomach, pats it and explains about Sara's cooking. She doesn't look impressed and frowns, turning away like she hasn't heard him.

Ja, Sara keeps him and the dog fed on all her French concoctions. Quiches made with bacon, cheese and sour cream, and stews with mushrooms and carrots in them. Sometimes, when she's tired after a long day in the kitchen at the Red Sail, she just brings him fried fish and chips. Those are his favourite nights. She dips her chips in mayonnaise and eats them one at a time, listening as he tells her about his worries. Then he lets her practise her French on him. It doesn't seem to matter to her that he can't understand a word she's saying.

'I must get in the habit of sommer just speaking. Otherwise when I get there, I'll be too frightened, and I don't want people to laugh at me.'

'If they laugh at you, I'll bliksem them.'

'You'll be sitting in your boat.'

Hendrik shrugs. Ja, it's true.

'What are you going to do first, when you get to Paris?'

'First I'm going to go and see that painting.' Sara points to the Mona Lisa poster. 'She lives at the Louvre Museum with lots of other famous works of art and thousands of people coming to stare at her. But I think she must be lonely. No one smiles like that, all the time, if they're happy. It's a smile that's been stuck onto her, you know. I want to go and see her when no one else is around, when she thinks she's all alone, and see what her face looks like then.'

Hendrik doesn't know what Sara is talking about. It's a painting. And paintings don't change when people are out of the room. They are what they are, whether someone is looking at them or not. But Sara has her own ideas, and Hendrik lets her talk.

He wishes he could tell her about the visvrou. But she's a secret that he's kept to himself for so long, he can't share it with anyone else. He wouldn't know where to begin. And besides, Sara might just think he's crazy, and maybe he is. Although Sara can't be all that sensible herself, with all her talk of smiling and not-smiling paintings.

Instead, he shares a dream he had the previous night. In it, he was on the ocean paddling on a boogie board. Suddenly he saw, not very far away, a black baby bobbing on a piece of cardboard, like a flattened cardboard box. Immediately he tried to get to it. He abandoned the boogie board and started to swim-crawl, one arm looping in the water over the other, pulling himself forwards through the bitterly cold surf. But he can't get to the baby, the current won't let him, and all the while he can see that the box is growing soggier and soggier. He woke up before he saw what happened next.

'I have no fokken idea what that dream is about, Hendrik.'

Hendrik smiles and slurps the last coffee from his mug. 'Me neither. Scrabble tonight?'

'Oui.'

'That is Frans for yes.'

The next morning, when Hendrik and Jakkals arrive at the cottage, he finds that Xolani has already started work on *Amanda*. After a quick greeting, Hendrik goes inside to feed the visvrou and make cups of coffee. Closing the door behind him, he wonders if this seems rude to Xolani. But what can he do? He has a secret to protect. Besides, he's sure that visvrou wouldn't want any more mense knowing about her. Who knows what they might try to do to her.

He finds her sitting in his armchair. When he comes closer, he sees that she's scratching at her legs. There's something up with her, but he doesn't want to stare and he doesn't want to go too close. He goes into the kitchen, but from the corner of his eye, he watches. Ja, she's scratching. She lifts her dress higher and there's a flash of dull silver. Her scales? Is she growing back her fish scales? Hendrik wants to go closer to make sure he's not dreaming, but he's already been in the house long enough. He doesn't want Xolani to wonder what's going on and come and look for him.

Later, when Hendrik and Xolani are sitting under the boat, drinking the coffee he's made for them, Hendrik's thoughts keep returning to the visvrou. If her scales are starting to grow back on her legs, what does it mean?

He knows he must seem silent and distant to the other man. He's about to apologise when Xolani asks, 'My friend, I am helping you to repair this boat, regardless. Tell me, why do you need it?'

Hendrik puts his coffee cup down. He rubs his palms on his knees. 'I need to take someone home,' he replies finally.

Xolani nods. To Hendrik's relief, he doesn't ask who. Suddenly, he feels a pang of regret that he hasn't gotten to know Xolani better these past eleven years.

'Why didn't you go home for Christmas? Do you really never go back?' Hendrik has been wanting to ask Xolani this question for weeks, but only now feels he can.

'Ag, I haven't gone back in a long time.'

'Why?'

'Eish. It is complicated. I cannot go back now.'

Silence. Hendrik can tell from his friend's sad countenance that he's thinking melancholy thoughts.

That evening, after Xolani's gone home, Hendrik tries to observe the visvrou without making her feel uncomfortable. Ja, she's walking funny too, like her thighs are stuck together. He watches as she shuffles past him into the bathroom, landing with a loud splash in the bathwater.

With a sigh, Hendrik picks up the bucket. He'll go and

get her some fresh seawater, then he'll meet Sara for din-ner and their nightly game of Scrabble.

He's getting better at this word game of hers, he thinks as he walks the streets towards her house. Last game he nearly won, but then, with only a handful of pieces left in the bag, Sara managed a triple word score with 'zebras' – a lucky fluke, after Hendrik put down 'bra'. But that was that. They've started to spend every night together, and it feels good.

When they're lying side by side on her bed, Hendrik asks her, 'Do you think the dead still communicate with us? Xolani says that his people, they believe in dead ances-tors staying to watch and help. Anton hasn't spoken to me once. Not in all the years. Sometimes I go to his grave to talk, but I don't hear anything back. And nothing from Rebekkah either.'

'I don't know. When I got the cancer, I thought about it. Who I could come back and haunt … You were high on my list.'

She laughs and begins to cough.

'You know you shouldn't smoke if you had cancer.'

'Ag, jirre, I shouldn't do many things. But I've decided that I'm soos die katte. I have nine lives. I lost two so far, so I still have seven left. And you too, Hendrik. Xolani told me what happened by the reserve in November. That's why I tried to speak to you that day on the beach, when you ran away from me. He says you tried to walk into the water, and he swam in to save you.'

Hendrik is silent. He can hear Sara pulling on her cigarette, and see the red glow as she inhales. He doesn't know what to say. So that night in the water, back in November, the hands pulling him up – they were Xolani's? It was Xolani who saved his life?

'I thought it was a dream, or—'

'Nee, no dream. That man saved your life. You've had friends watching you in this village all along, even though you didn't deserve it, you selfish bastard, and were too blind to appreciate it.'

When Xolani arrives at the boat the next afternoon after school, Hendrik's waiting for him. He's just managed to get rid of Mrs Simons, who together with her daughter-in-law and two of her curious friends had gathered outside his house. These days, when he steps out in the morning to let the dog out and to go take a piss himself in the outside toilet, Mrs Simons has taken to waving at him. Today she gave him a plate of biscuits: 'To give you energy when you're working on your boat.'

'Môre!' Xolani comes down the path in his blue work overalls.

'Molo, Xolani.' Hendrik's been waiting to see his friend again so he can greet him properly. 'Um … fok, man. I've forgotten the rest.'

'That is fine. A good start.'

Then Hendrik blurts out what's been on his heart and mind: 'Sara told me. It was you that night. Who saved me from drowning … I thought maybe I dreamt it. I was very drunk. But I want to say thank you.'

Xolani looks up. 'Anyone would've done the same. I couldn't let another man walk into the water and just drown.'

'But how did you know?'

'I had been watching you for a very long time. Ever since Rebekkah disappeared. Some months you seemed all right. But some months, very angry, very sad. That week, I saw, you were very angry.

'So I had been keeping an eye on you. Not too close, but just when I saw you looking very depressed or you were going too often to buy wine by the liquor store. So that day I saw. I saw you drunk in town. I saw your fight at the one-stop shop. I thought to myself, he is very bad today. Very sad. That night I could not sleep. A voice told me, go and check on him. When I arrived at your place, you were trying to lock the dog in the house, but she was barking barking, so you let her go with you. I followed.'

Hendrik cocks his head towards Jakkals, who's sleeping on a blanket in the sun. He can't look at Xolani. He feels a wave of shame.

'I have been behaving very foolishly.'

Xolani shrugs. 'Long ago, I was not very good for my family. I drank too much and stayed away. In you, I saw a man that I recognised.'

This is the first time Xolani has spoken about his family. Hendrik realises with another wave of shame that he's never asked Xolani anything about them.

When they stop for lunch, Hendrik opens his lunchbox and offers half to Xolani. He's wondering if Xolani is offended that he doesn't invite him inside, but if he is, he never shows it. Together they sit on chairs in the sunshine and eat polony sandwiches and drink Creme Soda.

'Where is your family now, Xolani?'

'They're still in the Eastern Cape. My wife and my daughter stay by Port Elizabeth.'

'When did you last see them?'

'Eish. More than ten years—'

Hendrik would like to ask what happened, to keep Xolani apart from his family for so long. But he can see from the way Xolani's screwed up his face in concentration that he's not yet ready to talk about it. Okay. Hendrik will not push. He picks up a sheet of sandpaper and begins to rub vigorously at a deck plank.

'Visvrou? Are you sleeping? What happened to Xolani, hey? You know? I bet you know, only you're not telling. I want to help him, visvrou, like he helped me. He saved my life. Did you know that? I thought that maybe it was you who pulled me up from the water that night, but you've known the truth about that all along too, I suppose. Jissus, you don't give much away. All right, okay. But I want to help him, so will you let me know what I can do? Will you? Please? I'll leave it with you. Just think about it. And another thing … Look, I don't like to ask, after what happened, you know, with me being drunk. But I need your help, visvrou, with Sara. You see, I think that maybe she and I, maybe we could start something, and even be happy. Only I don't know how to talk to her about it, and each time I think maybe I'll kiss her – and then each time something stops me, you know? I don't want to make any more mistakes or risk the friendship. I know she liked me in the past, but that was long ago and she hasn't said anything now or even tried to seduce me.

'Anyway, you're the one who can work magic. I'll leave it with you. Maybe you can show me what to do? Please visvrou, will you think about it?'

CHAPTER TWENTY-TWO

A TEENAGE AFRICAN BOY is herding cattle over a green hill. The cattle have long horns and their skin is a beautiful patchwork of white, brown and black. Down below, there's a shallow estuary, and across the estuary other cattle are lying on the sand. One cow is licking another's flank. They are peaceful and quiet, enjoying cool indigo-coloured shade. Beyond them, there's a patch of scrubby mangrove forest, and a goat tearing leaves off branches with teeth. The goat's pupils are not round. They are the shape of rectangles.

Hendrik's delighted to find that if he just flaps his arms slowly like a seagull's wings, he can go up and up until he's cruising high above. If he goes too high, he blows out out and out and feels himself slowly lower, like a hot-air balloon. If he wants to go up again, he need only flap his arms, once, twice, three times and again he's airborne. It takes some practice in the dream to get this balance right. Also, going forward is not so easy, but eventually he gets the hang of it. He hovers above the scrap of forest and watches the goat munching.

He moves back towards the boy, who's wearing a red T-shirt and is dreaming himself – of soccer, and of what might be beyond the ocean. If there are boys just like him with cattle and goats to tend, and no electricity at nightfall. Above him, a lighthouse stands solemn and patient.

Hendrik flaps his arms, and finds that he can float so high he can see across continents and oceans. And there, all the way on the other side, hundreds and hundreds of people are crowding into boats, some no larger than his bakkie boat. In one, a woman wraps her child in a blanket so that she can't see the waves rising up around. The woman's and the girl's heads are full of booming noise. Of fire, of shattering bricks and mortar and clouds of concrete dust and fear. They hear this still, though those things are far away now, and the only sound is the wind and the boat's diesel engine, straining against the sea. They too are heading towards a lighthouse. Below the lighthouse, a woman in jeans and a red jersey, who's never seen them before, never even met or spoken to them, is waiting to welcome them with blankets and bowls of steaming soup.

When Hendrik wakes up, he can still see the red-and-white-candy stripes of the lighthouse, the red of the woman's jersey and the boy's T-shirt. He can see into the

giant lighthouse lantern. In the corners are the powdered
wings of hundreds of dead moths, drawn to the light but
burnt to papery dust.

Lighthouses. Hendrik must teach visvrou about the vuurtorings. That way, if she gets lost or they get separated
when they're on their sea journey, they'll eventually be
able to find each other again. The lighthouses are to act as
his beacons to guide the way, in the day, when they can be
spied through a pair of binoculars, but also at night or in
fog, when he intends to follow their warning moans. But
first Hendrik must try to remember all the vuurtorings
between here and his destination on the Transkei coast.
This is what he tells himself as he packs up his tools after
another day of repairing the boat. He can't leave them
outside or even in *Amanda*. Skollies. Thieves. No, he must
lock them away each night in the tool hokkie at the back
of his house, and then unpack them again every morning.

His father was made to memorise all the lighthouses
and their unique flashes by his own father, who'd worked
on ships that delivered cargo further afield. When Hendrik's pa was sixteen, he ran away to go join the huge
Merchant Marine vessels transporting asbestos and steel
between South Africa, America and the Far East. He
went on as a galley boy. Bottom rung. All day long, he
peeled potatoes and scrubbed pots. He had his heart set
on one day climbing the ladder and ending up a steward
in an ironed white jacket and white gloves, serving the
officers at table.

'White gloves. They had the clean and easy jobs,' Pa spat, 'and they always helped themselves to the leftover food – turkey, beef, pudding, you name it.'

Then it happened. The First Steward cornered him one day when he was polishing in the galley. He pressed himself up against the boy, and Hendrik's pa could feel the bulge between the man's legs. He'd done two weeks collecting cargo, Durban to Cape Town. He jumped ship right then and there. And went back home to the village.

'You could have seen the Americas,' Anton said.

'Fok America. Ship of fokken moffies. I wasn't going to stay.' Although the First Steward was a married man, with a wife and children waiting for him back home.

'He was just looking for an excuse. Your father is not one for adventure.' That's what Auntie K said when the story came up again one Sunday after lunch.

When Hendrik told Sara the story a few nights ago, she only folded her arms and said simply, 'You must stop saying "fokken moffie". It's very prejudiced, Hendrik.'

Anyway, whatever happened to Pa on that ship, he made Hendrik memorise the lighthouses. It was knowledge that he wasn't going to waste.

'Do you know about lighthouses, visvrou? If we get separated at sea, you must look for them. If you follow them, you'll find your way to Mbashe Lighthouse. That's near where you come from. If we get separated. If there's a storm or something happens, you must make your way there. I'll wait for you there and you must wait for me. Or you don't have to wait for me. But I will wait for you there.'

She's looking at him. Watching him very closely, as she's been doing the past few days. She seems to be waiting for him when he gets home each time, and once or twice he's turned around to find her standing just behind him, a low hiss escaping her lips. He doesn't know what to make of it.

'This is important. Please pay attention,' he pleads.

He wants to help her. To make sure she makes it. He wants to make things right. But it's hard. The other day, he came home and she'd pulled all the blankets and sheets off his bed and left them in a heap in the kitchen. She'd also smashed the cake Sara had baked for him.

Hendrik looks at her. She's closed her eyes now and is shivering in the armchair. With a shudder, she pulls the blanket more tightly around herself. Under the dress, which she scratches at more and more, there are those beautiful, strong scales, which glisten whenever light catches them. Ja, she's started to grow her scales back for sure. So she must be ready to go. Her body is wanting to be back in the ocean.

'I will be in the boat, see, but you'll be in the ocean. It's better that way.'

He also wants to prepare her for what they might find when they finally reach her estuary. 'When you get home, you know, to your ikhaya. It may not be like you remember it. Everything may be different. And you may feel different because you've been living on land these past months. Sometimes people are cruel. Even our own people. Sometimes—'

He thinks about the night when he was drunk. He thinks about Rebekkah and Jarrad, and Lattie. He thinks about his father when he was in one of his moods. 'Sometimes even people who love us or loved us once or who we love, can be cruel. Maybe after being away so long, your own people won't welcome you. But if that happens, you must sommer make a plan. Only you musn't come back here. You do not belong here. I mean, you know you don't belong here, right? All day long all you do is watch that blerrie television or look at that scrap of newspaper and sigh about your home. And I think you're maybe getting sick. So you must go back. Only, I want you not to expect too much. I don't want you to be disappointed.'

Her eyes are open again and she's staring into the distance, hands neatly folded in her lap. She's staring elsewhere, but he thinks she's listening.

'Visvrou, luister. I'm sorry, okay? I'm sorry about what happened between us that night. I was angry and I was drinking too much. What I tried to do was very very wrong. It was terrible. I won't do it again. But I'm trying to help you now, so you're going to have to trust me. Please try to remember what I'm going to show you. I do ...' Hendrik hesitates. 'I do want what's best for you, visvrou.'

Hendrik unrolls the chart again. 'We people, we human people, we need to make charts like this. Some people use GPS, but I've heard stories. The GPS says there's no sand bank, but there is. Before you know it, you're in groot kak.'

The visvrou looks down and frowns at the charts.

'Ja, I know what you're thinking. What can these do

for you, a woman of the rivers and oceans, right? But you got lost, didn't you? Ja, you got lost and ended up here with me, so it will do you good to pay attention to what I'm going to teach you.' Hendrik clears his throat before continuing. 'These charts are what is accurate. We humans we like to record and try to control things. Most of the time we can't. But these charts, these are something you can trust. They'll help me get you to where you come from, and it will help us if we get separated.'

The water woman turns and looks out the window. Okay, so you're not going to make this easy for me, Hendrik thinks. But he won't give up. He points to the charts again. 'So here's how it's going to work, vis maiden. We're going to follow these lighthouses, the ones marked like this, all around the coast. From here, this is our lighthouse, to there.' Hendrik points to the lighthouse nearest to Mthatha. 'Our lighthouse is all white except it has a red cap. It flashes every fifteen seconds. So you could count, one elephant, two elephants, fifteen times.' Does she even know what elephants are? 'You've probably never seen one. They are groot things with a long trunk, like a hosepipe, like a long piece of seaweed, only grey. But it's the word that matters. The time it takes to say "elephant" is almost one second. That's what is important.'

Hendrik doesn't want to confuse her. He moves on. 'From here, we'll go south towards Cape Town. You know the way? It's how you got here, I think.' He shows her the next lighthouse to look out for. Hendrik has lots of details he wants to share with the water maiden. He doesn't want her to mistake the wrong lighthouse for the one nearest her home. It takes him almost an hour to go through them all, explaining each one's unique features. By the end of it, she looks like she might be nodding off. With a sigh, Hendrik gets up and fetches her a crayfish. Then he pins the chart to the wall in the bathroom, so she can see it even from her bath. 'I'm putting this up here so you can study it.' He's drawn each lighthouse as best he can with a red Koki pen. Beside each lighthouse, he also puts a number representing the lamps' flashes.

Then he goes to the fridge and takes out a Creme Soda. He likes its green. It's Sara's favourite green too, she tells him, and her favourite drink. Okay, he knows it's full of chemical kak, but he doesn't care. Sara has said he can come round later for a game of Scrabble and a plate of mince and rice. She's taking a break from making her French kos, she says, and Hendrik for one is relieved.

The other night, when Xolani came for dinner too, she presented them each with a plate of lettuce topped with a funny-looking cheese that stank like vrot feet. While she was in the kitchen fetching the bread, Hendrik leaned close to Xolani as they both looked down at their plates in dismay, and whispered, 'I hear in Frankryk the people eat snails—'

Xolani pushed at the stinking cheese with his knife. 'In my culture, Hendrik, people eat Mopane worms. So be grateful we are not at my uncle's place in Limpopo.'

Still, the food aside, he's come to cherish his time with Sara.

When she first told him about Scrabble, he'd been in-credulous. Scrabble? What the fok is Scrabble?

'It's a game. You make words with letters and earn points.'

'No ways, man. I won't play.'

'Come on. Don't you want to improve yourself, you blerrie lazy bastard?'

'I can't spell.'

'Neither can I. If you sommer make up a really good word, I'll let you keep it, but you must explain to me what it means.'

'Hmmm. Okay. All right. I'll do it.'

Ja, he's going to miss spending time with Sara. She won't be back from the Red Sail yet – night shift. Until she gets home, he'll rest – try to lift some of the weariness and ache off his bones. He goes to sit outside in the set-ting sun.

Yes, he could use GPS to navigate his way to the visvrou's home, that's what many people do these days. But the ocean and coast and its contours are in Hendrik's bones. He knows this shoreline better than he knows the lines of his own face. And beyond this coast, well, he'll just follow his gut and the lighthouses. If he keeps the boat always in sight of land, he shouldn't have too much trouble. Of course he'll use the GPS too. He's no expert in plotting a course us-ing charts, even though old Pete showed him years ago. And if fog rolls in, he'll just follow the old fisherman's rule: if you can hear the waves breaking on the shore, then you're in groot kak. Too close to those rocks, about to meet disaster.

Sometimes, when he used to run his hands over Rebekkah's body, he tried to memorise its contours, so they'd enter his skin, his bloed, as deeply as this shoreline. But he knows now that Rebekkah was a country he never really knew. He was like those dof whites long ago, landing in America and thinking it was China or India.

But he doesn't want to stew over such things now. He leans back and closes his eyes so that he can enjoy the last warm rays. He recalls the conversation with Xolani earlier in the day. Because it's a Saturday, Xolani wasn't expected to be at the school, so they worked on the hull of *Amanda* all day. The propeller was unscrewed and taken off, its rust removed and metal oiled. After two hours of solid work varnishing the bow, their backs ached and they were sharing a hard-earned pot of coffee. When Xolani turned to pass him a cigarette, the question just popped out of Hendrik's mouth: 'Why? Why are you not close to your wife and child?'

And to Hendrik's surprise, Xolani told him.

'I was not a good husband or father. I'd take my pay packet and go and spend it at the taverns, or on betting on the soccer or rugby. When my daughter was born, I didn't take responsibility for my child. I wanted freedom. Sometimes we behave in this way. It is not right. We leave burdens on the shoulders of our wives and mothers; the burden of providing and raising our children. My wife got sick from all the stress. She contracted TB. She took medicine and got better. But it was too late. I tried to convince her I was a changed man, that I'd found Jesus and now she could lean on me, but she would not take me back into our home. So I came here to look for work.'

There is silence between the two men as Xolani takes another sip from his cup.

'Tell me something, Xolani, what is your wife's name?'

'Noluthando.'

'Nol-oo-than-doo'

'Ja, sharp. Your Xhosa is getting much better.'

Hendrik smiled as Xolani dabbed the bow with more varnish. 'It's a pretty name. What is she like?'

'A good woman. Beautiful. She can find a better man than me, but I hear from my sisters that she still stays by herself. There is no other man in her life.'

'And your daughter?'

'My daughter, Vuyo, is clever. She is by the varsity in PE. She's doing studies linked to business. Every month I send money to help her, and I have hopes that she will go far and get a good job. Although I have been worried, what with the violent protests that happened on campus last November. I am worried that such students could jeopardise my daughter's plans.'

Hendrik sits and listens while Xolani speaks. He can hear the pain in his friend's voice. 'Have you not spoken to them in ten years too?'

'We speak on the telephone, but my wife does not want to see me and she does not want my daughter to see me either. I think she does not want Vuyo to be disappointed by me. She has grown used to not having a father.'

Hendrik nods. He imagines that must be very hard. To

be a father, but not to be able to see your child. To not watch her grow up or know what's happening in her life. But he also knows that, if Noluthando hasn't yet found another man to replace Xolani, even after all this time, then there is hope for his friend.

Hendrik lights another cigarette and looks at *Amanda*. Fok, she's a lekker boat. The first stars have begun to wink in the sky and the sight of them reminds him how, when he was a kid, one of the stories that Anton told him was that babies started as stars that flew down into a woman's stomach.

He wonders what sort of father he might have been if Rebekkah had agreed to have a child with him after all. Of course he wanted a son most of all, but son or daughter, he thinks he would have been happy. Hendrik sucks on the cigarette. Ja, Anton, if it was a boy, Anel, if it was a girl. But he never got either. And now he's too old. He will never have children. Never know what it's like.

Maybe it's for the best, since he doesn't seem to be able to properly care for even himself. He takes a last drag on the cigarette. He should go to Sara.

Still, he thinks, as he twists the cigarette butt under his shoe, it would've been nice to be a father. Ja. He mustn't lie to himself. It would have been something wonderful.

CHAPTER TWENTY-THREE

SARA AND HENDRIK go up the lighthouse together. It's a clear day, and the sky is that soft blue of a baby's blanket as they climb together right to the top, to the lantern room. Sara stands with her nose squashed against the glass, her breath fogging it.

'Sjoe, I haven't been up here since, I can't remember. Do you think it's a bit like this when you look down from the Eiffel Tower?'

Suddenly Hendrik wants to kiss her. But he doesn't. Instead he steps closer and takes her hand. Without turning to look at him, she threads her fingers between his. They stand for a long time saying nothing, just looking down on the village and the landscape that has been both of their homes their whole lives.

Why does he enjoy her company so much? Is it because she's familiar and comfortable? He doesn't have to impress her or be anyone but himself. After all, they've known each other since they were just snot-nosed kids.

There's something. Something about her. She has none of Rebekkah's obvious beauty. Her education. But there is something. Holding her hand, he feels like he's plunging his roots into deep and fertile ground.

But still, neither of them seems able to commit to one another, or even take the jump and just become lovers. Once or twice, he thought Sara was going to talk to him about such things. But nothing was said, or she started to talk about love and lovers, and then changed the subject to speak of other things. Ja, they never talk of love or the future. They never speak of the future at all. He wonders if this is because they've both learnt that the future cannot be trusted.

Ja-nee, Hendrik tells himself as he holds Sara's hand. From now on, all he's going to trust is this minute and the next and the next. Each one as it comes, and not think about what might be promised around the corner.

That night, when Hendrik sleeps by Sara's place, they do not break the unspoken vow of chastity that seems to have settled on them. But for the first time, when they climb into bed together, they do so naked. Hendrik feels shy at first, but then he gently runs his fingers over Sara's body, closing his eyes so that he can learn the contours of her, like a sailor memorising a seachart. When he comes to where he knows the great scar is under her left breast, he stops.

'Does it hurt?' he whispers.

Sara shakes her head, but there are tears in her eyes. Hendrik leans in and kisses the places where the surgeon's knife once cut in order to save Sara's life.

Later, she holds him close and asks him about that night when they came for Anton. It's a story she doesn't know. No one does. It's a story he's guarded with shame, and buried so deep that it feels like a tumour, but one that no operation could ever cut out.

'What happened that night, Hendrik? Please. I would like to know.'

And so he tells her.

It was April 1986. Varsity holidays. They had come for a week, five of them, all friends of Anton's from the Coloured varsity. All involved in the struggle. Something was brewing. Something was being planned, but Hendrik didn't know what, because Anton would not speak to him about it. He wouldn't even introduce Hendrik properly to these varsity friends of his. They didn't stay at the cottage. Instead, they all went to stay by Auntie K, who'd collected them from varsity in her car.

When Hendrik closes his eyes, he can still see each and every one of their faces. He can see them as if they were standing right in front of him. One of them, the tall one who always wore sunglasses, had brought a boom box, and whenever Hendrik went to Aunt K's there was music playing: jazz, or angry black rap from America you couldn't buy in the shops here, so Hendrik wondered where the tall, thin student had got them from. He himself had a Walkman by then, and listened to Michael Jackson and Stevie Wonder.

Every day, after coming back to shore and completing his chores, Hendrik would knock on the door and shout for Anton. But he was sent away.

'I'll come visit you and Ma by the house when I can, but we're talking here. You can't come inside. We're talking about important things. We will need your help. But not yet.'

Through the cracked-open door, Hendrik saw stacks of paper with black and red writing. A typewriter too.

'We're writing textbooks,' the young man with sunglasses said. 'Real textbooks to educate kids like you, ones that speak and teach the truth.'

The other men laughed, but not Anton. He shook his head. As if his friend had already said too much and he didn't want Hendrik involved.

When Hendrik passed the house at night – ja, he was spying on them, jealous about being left out – the lights were always on and so was the music, and the curtains were permanently drawn. They seemed never to sleep. Creeping up to the window, he could hear nothing but music. Auntie K kept them fed, and more than once he saw them all sitting on the beach with beer bottles in their hands, even though drinking on the beach was against the law. And she squashed all rumours in the village, or tried to: 'They're just students come to take a holiday by the sea. Stop with all the skinner!'

Because there was gossip. These were troublemakers,

come from the varsity to stir up protest in the community. A State of Emergency had been declared. Schoolchildren were rioting, burning down schools and toyi-toyiing through township streets. The police might even be after them.

And then it happened. Anton and his friends had been in the village maybe ten days. Everything was quiet. An ordinary day. A boring night. Ma had been feeding Pa with a spoon by the hospital. He'd had his stroke by then and could not look after himself. When she came home, she was moeg and Hendrik made her a cup of tea. Bedtime. Sleep. Hendrik lay in bed listening to his Walkman. Michael Jackson. Thriller. *Thrii-ller-night*! The singer's high voice shouted in his ears and Hendrik imagined himself breakdancing on concrete. His hand was going down to his piel to maybe break the boredom, when the sweep of car lights rolled across the walls of his room and through the house. The sound of cars stopping and doors opening. They left the engines on. Many feet crunching over the ground towards the front door. And then bang bang bang. 'Polisie! Maak oop!'

'Waar is hy?' The policeman barked at his mother. Her tiny frame was rigid with terror. The policeman was standing so close that the tips of his black boots were touching her toes.

Hendrik was frightened for his mother. He was frightened for himself. 'He is by Auntie K,' Hendrik shouted, 'writing textbooks!'

The policeman looked at Hendrik and walked over to

him, but Ma ran to him too. She stood between Hendrik and the policeman.

'Asseblief, my baas, hy's net 'n kind. He does not know what he is speaking about.'

Without a word, the policeman took Hendrik's ma by the shoulder and gently but firmly moved her to the side. Hendrik stood gazing up into the blue eyes of the devil himself.

'What are they doing there? Writing textbooks?'

'Ja, Meneer,' Hendrik croaked, 'to give to the school-children.'

Hendrik felt his mother's hand grip his arm. Each fingernail dug into his flesh like burning coals. It was too late. He'd given Lucifer what he needed.

The policeman summoned an inferior to him. He whispered into this man's ear. Without a word, they all left.

Later, Hendrik heard that Anton and his friends had been planning on inspiring Coloured high-school kids across the Western Cape to rise up like the black ones were doing in Johannesburg. They were putting together plans. Documents to help inspire revolt. They would've wanted Hendrik's help. After all, he was still at high school, about to start Standard 9, although he'd drop out before the end of that academic year.

Sara listens as Hendrik speaks, and all along she says nothing. Just strokes his hair.

'Do you think it was my fault they got him? When they

threatened Ma, I told him where they were. At Auntie K's house. And I told them what the one man had said, about the textbooks. Maybe they could have gotten away if it wasn't for me.'

Sara is silent for a long time. When she speaks, her voice is soft and gentle. 'Hendrik, you were just a boy. Jissus, just a frightened child. And your brother, he made his own choices. The time has come to try to let go of the sorrows and anger of the past.'

CHAPTER TWENTY-FOUR

'XOLANI, I WANT TO TELL YOU A STORY I've only told one other person in the whole world.'

And with that, he repeats the story he told Sara the previous night. About Anton. About the police. About his fear that he let his brother and family down.

Xolani listens in silence, his face creased with sympathy.

'But I'm telling you this not so you'll feel sorry for me. I'm telling you this so you'll know that we all make mistakes and some are really terrible. But you have to forgive yourself. Just go and see your wife. Go and see her and look her in the eyes and say, "I'm sorry. I made a fokop, but I am sorry and I love you." She must still love you if she's never gone with someone else.'

'No, never. She is a good Christian woman. She does not believe in breaking her marriage vows.'

'Just go, before it's too late. I wish I'd had the chance to say I was sorry to my brother. I don't even know if he knew it was me who betrayed him to the police. I didn't mean to ... but that doesn't matter. What's done is done. Go and make peace with your wife and child while you still can.'

Xolani stands and says nothing. Hendrik can see he's really considering it. And so this is the moment Hendrik's been waiting for.

'I will take you, Xolani. I will take you on *Amanda* to your wife and daughter in PE. It's on my way to the Transkei anyways. We must stop there to get more diesel and supplies. So you won't be alone. I'll even rent a car and drive you to their door if you want—'

A real smile. Deep. One that shines from the eyes. But still, Xolani says nothing apart from, 'I need to go away and think about what you have said.'

The next morning, when Hendrik comes out of his cottage to begin work on *Amanda*, he finds Xolani waiting for him.

'Okay, my friend,' Xolani tells him. 'I will do it. I will go with you.'

After this, something changes between the two men. The shyness that Hendrik often felt in Xolani's presence evaporates. All afternoon they talk and talk, sharing stories and jokes, even after it's too dark to work any longer on *Amanda*. Xolani talks about how he met his wife at a cousin's funeral. And Hendrik talks about how he met

Rebekkah at the village basaar. Then Hendrik tells Xolani about Rebekkah and Jarrad.

'Are you certain?'

'Ja, I think so. Sara saw them, and Jarrad has confessed that he was in love with her.'

Xolani shakes his head. 'I'm very sorry, my friend. In my culture, if a nephew did such a thing, he would have to face the elders.

'Ja well, here there are no elders left. If Auntie K was still alive, she'd have known what to do with him. She would have set it all straight and bliksemed him proper, but she's long buried in that graveyard with my parents and Anton, and there are no others to take her place.'

'It is sad what is happening with the young in this country. I feel it too when I see what is happening even in this village. They do not respect their elders like they should and many have lost their way.'

Hendrik nods. 'It's true. But things must change. They can't go on like this.'

A long silence. Hendrik can't see Xolani's expression. Only the red glowing tip of his cigarette as he inhales.

'Come, shall we go? Sara is expecting us,' Xolani says at length.

'Ja, she'll be baking one of her French upside-down snail koeks.'

Sara's waiting for them. Deliberately, she's a little off with Hendrik. She wants him to know that she's upset, to maybe ask her some questions so she doesn't have to just come out with it. But Hendrik doesn't even notice. She can see he's tired. He quickly sinks into the normal routine of eating the food she's prepared and then setting up the Scrabble board with Xolani. This has been their ritual for weeks now.

Sara tries to act normal and concentrate on the game. This thing has been troubling her all day, but now that Hendrik's here, she doesn't know how to say it. Even when Xolani finally goes home (and she loses on purpose so that their friend will go home sooner), she cannot find the words.

After all, how does she tell Hendrik that this morning, when he was buying more screws for the boat or out on the sea or something, she passed by the cottage and saw a woman's face peering out of the window? A black woman's face. Inside Hendrik's plek. Staring right at her.

It would sound mal. But something has started to stir in her. Questions about all these months when he hasn't let her inside his cottage, even though they've become close. Not once. She lies next to him, listening to the slow rhythm of his exhausted breathing and the snoring of the dog. Finally, she's slipping into sleep. But there is a feeling like poison in her chest.

CHAPTER TWENTY-FIVE

ONE DAY AND THEN ANOTHER PASSES. And each night, Sara is haunted by the same terrible dream. A woman. Young. Dark skinned. Beautiful. In Hendrik's arms. In the dream, he's kneeling just like she saw Jarrad kneeling at the feet of Rebekkah. And then there's the sound. In the dream, the woman opens her mouth, and the sound that comes out is so terrible, worse than nails down a chalkboard, that Sara wakes each night with a start. That's what has happened again tonight. The dream. The scream. And now Sara is lying awake again while the rest of the village sleeps, including the snoring Hendrik.

She imagines him in the dark. His eyes closed. His face at peace. She thinks about how old he's gotten, and what he was like when they were children. Often up to mischief, always in the shadow of his brother. But even then, she knew she loved him. He's a man who needs a woman's help. She can't believe he wouldn't have told her if there was another woman staying by his place. She'll go today, when he's working on *Amanda*, and one way or another force him to let her go inside to see for herself. She's sure her mind is playing games with her.

When Hendrik wakes, he climbs out of bed and goes to the toilet, pulling at his pyjama broeke as he walks. Sara's already dressed. She's been sitting in the room, watching him and waiting for him to wake up too.

'You working on *Amanda* today?'

'Ja, ja. Last bit of greasing.'

Good. She'll make a plan to slip out of the Red Sail in the morning. She doesn't have her break until 3 p.m., after the lunchtime rush, but Pearl will cover for her. Sara has considered calling in sick, and watching Hendrik and the house from afar until a good moment comes to have a snoop. But she's changed her mind. Why think the worst, she tells herself; just make an excuse to get inside.

She hears the toilet flush and picks up her purse. 'I'll come by your place with some lunch.'

'Dankie,' Hendrik calls back from the bathroom. There's the sound of teeth brushing.

By 10 o'clock, Sara can't wait any longer. In spite of her wish to trust Hendrik, she has that terrible feeling in her stomach again, and the memory of her dream is circling in her mind, thud thud like a washing machine. She packs some fish and chips and tells Pearl she must go home quickly. Time of the month, and she's forgotten to bring pads. Pearl tells her not to worry. If Mr Rodriguez asks where she is, a mention of rooikappie will be enough to silence him. That's how it is with most men and such things. It seems to scare the kak out of them.

Sara hurries down the main road and turns down the street that leads to Hendrik's place. Before she can see him, she can hear him. The bang bang of nail on wood. Good, he's home.

'Môre, Hendrik.'

'Môre-môre. You've come early. Everything all right?'

Hendrik looks concerned. He can't have failed to notice that she's not been herself the past few days. A bit irritable and much more quiet than usual.

Sara passes him the parcel. 'Ja, all fine. Listen, Hendrik, I need to go inside and use your bathroom.' Sara lowers her voice. 'It's my time of the month.'

Hendrik turns and picks up some more nails. 'Ja, of course, but you know where the toilet is.' He indicates the outhouse at the back of the cottage.

Sara shakes her head. She's watching the cottage, and thinks she sees a twitch behind one of the kitchen curtains. 'Nee, I've had an accident. I need to wash … You understand—'

Hendrik turns to face her. Is it in her imagination, or does he look worried?

'Um, ek is jammer, but my water isn't working.'

'What do you mean?'

'Ja, strange thing. Problem with the pipes. No water in the house. Why don't you just go home? It's not so far.'

Another twitch behind the curtain, or is Sara's mind playing tricks? She can feel her heart starting to beat faster. 'I'll make a plan, Hendrik. Please just let me inside.'

Sara steps towards the front door. But Hendrik steps forward too. He will not let her pass. 'Please, Sara. There is no water. Just go home and do it there. Or go to Mrs Simons. She won't mind.'

Without a word, Sara turns and leaves.

When Hendrik gets home, it's very late and Sara's already in bed. She's left him a note on the table next to a plate of food, saying that she's not feeling well and can he please not disturb her.

Hendrik reads the note and sits down to the food. It's leftovers. He wonders what's up with her, but he also knows women can be strange when their time of the month has come, although that's not usually Sara's way.

Ja, she was upset about not being let into the house today. He wonders if she's starting to get suspicious, and what he can do about that. He's already started to worry about how he'll get the visvrou to the boat on the morning they must leave. He'll have to do it very early, while everyone's still asleep and it's dark and the beaches deserted. He'll lead her to the water and tell her to wait for him and the boat, and follow when it passes. Maybe it's even better to take her to the cove at the reserve and tell her to wait in the water there.

He sticks his fork in a potato and tastes it. It needs salt, but he eats it anyways. He's too moeg to move – if he could eat and sleep at the same time, he would. After a few mouthfuls, he gives the rest to Jakkals. Stripped down to his vest and boxers, he climbs into bed beside Sara. The room is dark and he can feel the slow movement of her chest rising and falling, rising and falling. He wants to roll over and stroke her face and smell the cigarette smoke in her hair. But he doesn't. Instead he rolls onto his other side and quickly tumbles into the pit of sleep.

Sara is awake. It must be long after midnight. It only took Hendrik a few minutes to go into a deep sleep, and she's grateful. It's taken all her self-control to lie here, pretending to sleep, when all she wanted to do was snatch his keys from him and march him to his cottage. But now that he's asleep, she'll go herself.

She sits up. That sickness feeling has been in her stomach all day. Sara can't get the thought out of her head: he's seeing a woman. She'd never asked him if there was someone else, because it was always Rebekkah Rebekkah Rebekkah. But has she been misreading him all this time?

And a black woman? Now Sara's no racist, but still, she can't believe it. But why else would he not let her in today? He was firm about it. And there was that twitching of the kitchen curtain, like someone was spying and listening.

And a face. Ja, she's sure she saw a face. An African face. Young. Beautiful. A domestic? No, Hendrik would never do such a thing – pay for his house to be cleaned. The truth is that she and Hendrik have still not slept together, and now she's starting to worry that she knows why. Maybe.

She listens. Ja. He's fast asleep as usual. Working so hard on the *Amanda* means that every night he just collapses, even though some nights she's worn the night shirt that shows a bit of shoulder and has even painted her toenails a seductive red. He won't even know that she's gone if she just slips out and has a little look around his house. She must just shake this mal, gnawing doubt, once and for all.

Very gently, Sara lifts up the covers. She mustn't wake up the brak, either, but really, she thinks the animal is deaf as a stick. Quickly she pulls a coat over her nightdress and buttons it up. Then she steps into her slip-slops and, without a sound, unlocks the door and goes out into the night. She moves silently along the deserted street, the streetlights guiding her down the hill towards his place.

She's sure she is mal – but ja, she has to go and find out. It's the dream that's making her do it. The dream she's had the last three nights. She'll just take a quick look and then she'll know for sure, and she can push these strange thoughts from her mind.

As she turns the corner, she can see the cottage in the distance. She's known that cottage her whole life, and now there's a For Sale sign on it. Jissus, Pinkie and Jarrad move fast. She knows that Hendrik sold it for the price of the new boat, plus a little extra, but that's a fraction of what it's worth and what those two will get from some rich white when they sell it on.

Naïve. That's what Hendrik has always been. First with

Rebekkah. She never really committed herself to him, even after they were married. Wouldn't even give him children, and never closed her heart to Jarrad. Ja, Sara feels a little bad for that story about them in the factory. But Rebekkah was no good, and even gone, she was killing Hendrik. Making him drink himself into an early grave as he waited for a woman who was never coming back.

As Sara approaches the house, she sees that behind the curtains there's the blue light of a television. Did Hendrik forget to turn it off? But then she knows. The woman. That staring black face. She is inside. Sara will go. She will confront her. She will get to the bottom of this.

But just as she thinks this, the front door opens and the woman steps out, like she's been waiting for Sara all along. Tall and slim, and she's wearing Rebekkah's yellow dress – Sara recognises it immediately. Sara stands stock still and watches. The woman closes the door behind her and then, as though she hasn't seen Sara (although she has), begins to move in the opposite direction, down the road that leads to the beach. She seems to be shuffling, like someone who's wearing a dress that's too tight, or has rope around her ankles. But in spite of this, she moves fast.

What should Sara do? A part of her wants to turn around and run home. But another part of her feels like the woman's calling her. That she's playing games with Sara, and wants her to follow. Okay. She will. Something about this woman makes Sara feel like she has no choice. She must follow like she followed Rebekkah that day to the factory. She'll do it for Hendrik. He must have gotten himself in to some sort of kak if a woman like this has been staying by his place and he hasn't even told her or Xolani.

Sara thinks there must be something wrong with her eyes, but each time the woman walks under a streetlight, she seems to glisten. Minute by minute, step by step, they're getting closer to the sea. Closer to the very place where, Sara realises when they pass the dark mansions with their blinking alarm lights, Rebekkah was last seen. But still Sara follows. She must get Hendrik. If this woman has him, she must get him back. What would these two have in common? So she follows. And the woman shuffle-walks. Never stopping, never turning back – but Sara knows that the woman knows that Sara is following her.

They reach the car park that in summer is full of tourists' cars as they walk on the beach. But now it's deserted. Then the low dunes. The woman walks over them. Her pace never changes. Sara follows. It's like an invisible thread ties them together, pulling, pulling. The streetlights are behind her now. Their warm orange halo. Soon Sara will not be able to see in the darkness. But she can hear the ocean and the seespoke. The woman is ahead, shuffling towards the water. Walking into the darkness. Taking Sara with her.

Sara feels the water sloshing around her ankles. They've reached the water. The woman can't be far ahead, but Sara can't see her. She was just here. Just in front. And now? It's too dark.

Sara feels despair. She feels the ocean gathering around her legs. But she can't turn back. This woman is calling her. Tormenting her. Deeper into the water Sara goes. The icy waves are splashing round her knees, and the hems of her coat and nightdress are getting wet. She's too far in, and she cannot swim. She's about to give up and turn back, when just then she sees the woman. Just in front. Glowing silver almost. Just a little deeper.

She calls out to her now: 'Hey, what are you doing by Hendrik's place? Who are you?'

She wants to grab this strange woman. To grab her and shake her. She reaches out. And as she touches her, Sara feels herself go under.

CHAPTER TWENTY-SIX

HENDRIK WAKES. He reaches out a hand to feel Sara sleeping safely beside him in the dark, but he finds nothing but blankets. Hendrik sits up and switches on the light and the night's dreams recede like a tide being pulled out. Sara? She's not in the bed. Through the curtains, the first soft orange light is seeping in. She must be in the kitchen, he thinks, getting ready to go to the early shift at the Red Sail. He throws back the covers and steps over the dog, which doesn't stir. Just then he hears a banging on the front door and the sound of Daryll's anguished voice. He's screaming Hendrik's name.

Hendrik and Xolani stand by the graveside. The last of the mourners have already made their way to the church hall for the refreshments, but the two men cannot move.

They stare at the wooden cross that marks the grave. If they had any tears left, they'd cry them now, but it feels like that's all they've done since they heard the news of Sara's drowning, and saw the scratched, grey body for themselves at the morgue.

Xolani repeats the question that's tormented them both this past week: 'I do not understand it. She was not a foolish woman. Why did she do it?'

Ja. Why? Hendrik clenches then unclenches his fists. After Daryll arrived, hysterical, at the house and told him what the fisherman had found washed up on the beach, he didn't go down there, where the ambulance was collecting the body. Instead he went to his place. Drove there in his sleeping vest and underpants and no shoes.

As soon as he parked the car, he saw fresh strands of seaweed and clumps of beach sand lying on the path. Had Sara come to the house? Had she seen the visvrou? Had the visvrou seen her?

When he pushed into the house, everything looked normal and quiet. He went straight to the bathroom. There was no sign of wet footprints. No sign that the visvrou had actually left the house. Nee, she was just doing what she'd mostly been doing these past two weeks: sleeping. Hendrik stood and watched her in the bath. The only sound was a sharp hiss as she exhaled.

Only then did he weep, sinking to the ground in the bathroom doorway.

'Visvrou, Sara has been in an accident. She has drowned. Why did she do it? You people know. You people can tell me. What happened? Why …?' He sobbed, and through his tears he thought he saw the visvrou smile. But when he blinked and looked again, her face was frozen in sleep as before, her mouth open as she hissed through her teeth.

She's stayed that way ever since. She hasn't left the bath once since that morning. And Sara? When he least expects her, she pops up. At the start of the funeral, he thought he saw her in the crowd, wearing a ridiculous purple hat, weeping at her own eulogy. When he looked again, she was gone.

Hendrik looks up. He half expects to see Sara jumping out from behind a tombstone. But there is only Xolani standing with his head bowed. Ja-nee, maybe the time has come to tell his friend about the mamlambo; and maybe about the new Sara ghost too. But he doesn't know what Xolani's reaction will be, and they're supposed to be leaving in ten days' time. The weather's already starting to cool, and Hendrik doesn't want to get caught out by winter storms that will make the voyage impossible. Ja-nee, Xolani has enough on his plate already, without trouble with water maidens and ghosts.

Anyway, grief does strange things to your mind. He knows. Maybe this new Sara ghost isn't really even there; maybe he's seeing what he wants to see. Or maybe it's Hendrik who's actually dead. Maybe he *did* succeed in drowning himself last November.

Still, just in case, he whispers out of the corner of his mouth: 'I won't break my promise, Sara.'

Xolani is murmuring a prayer, his head bowed.

'Is that why you keep on popping up?' He feels her standing next to him. When he opens an eye, he sees her golden shoes. She's come to attend the ritual.

Originally, the plan had been to do the ritual together. Him, Sara and Xolani. But after Sara's accident, Hendrik and Xolani decided to do it today, just the two of them, after her funeral. But Sara won't be left out. Even though she's just been buried, she can't be kept away.

Xolani begins. He tells Hendrik to close his eyes, and reads in isiXhosa from the Bible: 'Kuba iyaluthibaza uqh-withela, luthi cwaka, amaza azole, ibafikise eluchwebeni abalulangazelelayo.'

What is Xolani saying? Hendrik doesn't know. He can feel Sara beside him still. He opens an eye again and sees her fidgeting, stepping in and out of her gold high heels, which always seem to hurt her feet. Her hat is skew. Hendrik cracks open the other eye. His mustn't be angry. 'But fok, Sara, what were you thinking?'

Can Xolani hear him? Xolani's facing Sara's grave still, and Hendrik can see that his friend is crying. When he switches to English, Xolani's voice cracks, but still he reads. 'Psalm 107: "He maketh the storm a calm, so that the waves thereof are still. Then are they glad because they be quiet; so he bringeth them unto their desired haven." Baba, please help us. Please be with us on our journey and give us strength and courage, and lead us safely there to our destination, as once you led your peoples long ago across deserts. Amen!'

'Amen,' Hendrik choruses, more to please Xolani than anything else. His faith has never felt weaker. He thinks he hears Sara say 'Amen' too, but Xolani doesn't seem to notice.

Then there's another ceremony. A silent one. Xolani stands, his head bowed for a few minutes before he starts to sing, 'Siyakuuuuuduumisa Thixo ...'

When the singing is over, Xolani and Hendrik walk back towards the village, then down to the beach. One night, as they were packing away the Scrabble board, Sara had said she had a ritual of her own that she wanted them to do before the two men set off on *Amanda*. Wishes in a bottle. From her handbag she'd pulled out three empty cola bottles, paper and three pencils. 'Write what you like,' she'd told them, 'but it better include something about us all seeing each other again.'

Hendrik had saved the bottles when Villeen was clearing out Sara's house after the accident. Now, in silence, he and Xolani throw theirs and then Sara's into the water. Just then, a giant wave smashes itself against the rock, spraying foam and water like spit, drenching them both to the skin. Fok jou, ocean, Hendrik thinks as he turns. Again he thinks he sees Sara, just for an instant. Dancing on the rocks, her back to the sea.

It is to the Red Sail they go now. The last part of an afternoon of rituals they'd planned as a way to sprinkle good luck on their journey and beg the gods and ancestors for help.

'After every ceremony, a feast,' Sara had told them.

And it's a feast they tuck into at the Red Sail. Fried fish, and calamari and chips, and even some prawns which Sara's friend Leila sneaks into the combo without the boss seeing. Raising their cooldrinks, they toast adventure and friendship. But the truth is, neither Xolani or Hendrik has much appetite. They're only doing this to honour Sara, because it's what she would've wanted.

When Xolani leaves the table to go inside to buy cigarettes, Hendrik sits and looks at the swifts, gathering in the plane trees that line the road across from the restaurant. They cheep and chatter as they whirl on black wings. Soon they'll be flying elsewhere. North. Away from the approaching winter. Ja, my friends. You too. Soon we'll both be away from this place. Hendrik thinks of the money from Jarrad and Pinkie sitting in his bank account. No doubt, the estate-agent boards will come down as soon as he and Xolani are on *Amanda* and out of sight of the village. Traditional fishermen's cottages are selling for small fortunes to seasonal inkommers, and he's heard a rumour that a woman from Johannesburg made a cash offer without even seeing it. But he'd sold to Jarrad because he wanted it all taken care of quickly.

'You sold it too cheap.' Sara. She's back. She takes off her hat and puts it on the table.

'Well, you went and got yourself drowned.'

'Not me. Not me.' Sara pulls a piece of seaweed from her hair and drops it on the floor.

'What do you mean, not you not you? Speak sense, woman. I don't care if you're a real ghost or just something in my mind. What happened that night?'

But Sara's up again, moving away. 'Kom, Hendrik.' She offers him a hand. She wants them to dance, but when he shakes his head, she shrugs and floats back to the table. She grabs a handful of chips and pushes them into her ghost-mouth, licks her ghost-fingers.

'You know,' she tells him through another mouthful, 'I don't think I've ever felt more alive.'

'Don't speak kak, man. You're dead. You're dead and I'm left here, making you talk to me in my mind. I suppose you know about the visvrou now.'

'Don't talk to me about her. I don't want to fight.'

'I'm sorry I didn't tell you. I wasn't sure if she was real, and then I wasn't sure what to tell you. It's all been mal, man. I feel mal. Maybe you're both existing only in my imagination. Too much wyn. Too many years.'

But Hendrik knows, too, what Xolani has told him: that the ancestors speak to the living to guide them, even after the ancestors are dead. But they do it in people's dreams, Xolani says, and Hendrik is not sleeping now. He wonders why it's Sara who's come back to him like this, and not Anton or Auntie K or even his parents.

'I'm sorry I didn't kiss you when I was alive, or take you to bed,' she says.

'Ja, it would've been nice—' Hendrik takes a swig of cooldrink.

'Well, let's not dwell on the past. You know what works on my nerves about this village right now?' Sara asks, spearing a piece of Hendrik's fish with a plastic fork. 'There's not enough colour. I mean, why must all the houses be white? Once you and Xolani leave me in this place all alone, I've decided that I'm going to paint my cottage something bright.'

Villeen has already moved her good-for-nothing son and his children into it, but Hendrik decides he won't mention that to Sara.

'What will the council say about that?'

'Ja, one of them on the council was sitting by the Red Sail last month having a whisky. I went to him and said, "Meneer, why can't we paint our houses every colour of the rainbow? We are the rainbow nation, are we not?" That man had no sense of humour. He just shook his head and said, "You know that's not what is allowed. It's the law. It's got to be white."

'"Jinne, Meneer," I said, "that is very racist. And I thought apartheid was over." His eyes swelled up so big!' Sara holds up her ghost-hands as though they're holding oranges. 'Poor bastard, I had him worried.' Sara laughs, slapping her ghost-thigh at her own joke.

Her hair's different now. Pinned back with clips like it used to be before she had chemo and changed it. Hendrik squints at her. She doesn't even look pale or transparent or whatever else ghosts or ancestors are supposed to be. If it wasn't for the fact that they all buried her only a few hours ago, he'd think she was alive. Is it possible to be dead *and* alive at the same time?

There's a long silence.

'Are you scared?' Sara asks finally.

'Scared of what?'

'Leaving this village and just going off on your boat? I mean, you've been here your whole life.'

'Ja, a bit.'

Sara nods. 'Well, don't go and fokken drown on that new boat of yours. Some people might miss you, although it would mean we could have a reunion. If you play your cards right. You and me, in the afterlife.'

Hendrik looks at Sara. He knows his eyes have gone shiny with tears. She hands him a paper napkin.

'I'm not crying. There's just suddenly sand in my eyes.'

'Okay, all right. But I want to say, I miss you too. I miss you a lot.'

Xolani is approaching with his cigarettes. When he sees Hendrik's expression, he frowns. 'Are you all right, my friend?'

Hendrik nods, but he sinks his face into his hands.

CHAPTER TWENTY-SEVEN

EASTER SUNDAY. It's 8 a.m., and today's the day they are due to launch *Amanda* and take the visvrou home. Hendrik's standing on the beach in his yellow oilskins, looking at the temporary wooden launch they've built, which needs only to be pushed into the sea. *Amanda* is beside it, ready to be reversed onto it with Daryll's bakkie. She looks beautiful in her red and blue paint. The sky is still overcast with rain clouds, and the sea's a lead grey, except for the waves breaking rhythmically and gently on the shore, which are green. Visvrou-eyes green. Everything is ready for the journey – except that the visvrou, the one this journey was supposed to bring home, is gone. Sara's gotten rid of her.

At 4 a.m., Hendrik was woken by the sound of heavy rain playing on the roof. At first he thought he was maybe still dreaming. It was the first heavy rain he could recall since the drought began, more than ten months before. He lay in the dark and listened. The rain continued, drumming its fingers impatiently.

He opened his eyes. Was the visvrou listening to the rains too? Any sea creature knows that heavy rain, and the stormy waves it brings, makes the ocean impossible for a boat the size of *Amanda* to travel. But he'd promised her they'd leave in the morning. Only, how could they, if it was raining like this? He turned on the light, stepped over the dog and went to the bathroom. He wanted to reassure her: don't worry, I'm good as my word, I'll find a way to take you, even if the rain is throwing the ocean into a fit.

He turned on the bathroom light. 'Visvrou, moenie worry nie … we'll sommer maak a plan.'

But she was not awake and waiting for him. Nee. She was gone. The bath was dry, the plug pulled out. The seaweed in a bunch around the drain. The water woman was gone, and in her place, scrubbing out the slimy seaweed and kelp fronds, was Sara.

He didn't know what to say.

Sara simply shrugged. 'You couldn't have both of us. Ancestor or mamlambo. I showed her where she could take a jump. I'm stronger dead than I was alive.'

'Did she … was she the one who …?'

Sara shrugged again. 'Ag, all's fair in love and war.'

Hendrik felt his whole body start to tremble. 'Sara … I'm so sorry. I should have—'

'So she got me then and I got her now – and in the end I got *you*.'

'Are you saying that you're staying by me now?'

'Well, if I did and I could, it won't be mos a *conventional* relationship. But I suppose there would be benefits. Anyways, how can I ever leave you, Hendrik? Look at the kind of kak you get yourself into when I'm not around.' She pointed to the buckets of seaweed and the nasty brown tide ring on the inside of the bath, all that was now left of the visvrou. 'Ja, you're going to need me on that boat of yours. And besides, you'll never beat Xolani at Scrabble without my help.'

Hendrik watches a young blonde woman jog past in a zipped-up red fleece, her hair in a ponytail. The village is still quiet. The shops are closed and so are the restaurants. Only the churches are busy, and have been busy since before sunrise so that worshippers can welcome Christ on the morning of his Resurrection. When Hendrik drove past at 7 a.m., the hymns flowed out from the Anglican church's windows like sacred wine:

> *Jesus Christ is Lord*
> *You are Lord*
> *You are Lord*
> *You have Risen from the dead.*

Xolani is still by his church. Last night, he and Hendrik went through their supplies for the final time. Xolani had spoken of delaying the trip after the funeral. He said he was worried about Hendrik, that he thought his friend needed time to grieve and recover. But Hendrik had forced a smile, and said that he was feeling better and that the journey would do him good. And it was true. He hadn't seen Sara since the funeral and had worked hard to appear calm and even upbeat these past ten days, whenever he saw Xolani. That was until this morning in the bathroom.

Hendrik closes his eyes and inhales deeply. The air still smells a little of rain, even though the skies are now clear and the waters calm. Ja, it turns out the storm was not so wild after all. When he turns to look down the beach, he thinks he sees Sara approaching carrying a plastic bag. But he blinks and looks again, and sees it is a woman he doesn't know.

In his rucksack, he has her Scrabble board. It's the only thing he took from Sara's cottage – Villeen won't care. He and Xolani will play on the journey. They will play and think of Sara. When she was alive, Sara hadn't wanted to give him the game to take on their journey. She was superstitious: 'It's my lucky Scrabble board, you know. And anyway, you'd just go and lose the pieces in the sea, or that brak would eat them. And then what? You can't play Scrabble with no vowels.'

Hendrik nods. He feels tears coming again. But he doesn't want to cry. Not now. The woman passes. She looks nothing like Sara. Nothing at all. Hendrik watches her go, and clutches the Scrabble box tightly to his chest. Just then he senses a hand around his arm. Sara. She's back. Just like she promised. Going. But always coming back.

'You ready, Skipper?'

She's dressed in a stripy red, white and blue top, a red skirt and white flip-flops. Hendrik's glad she's wearing the colours of France again. Can ghosts travel on airplanes? Will she finally make it to Paris, now that she doesn't have to worry about Franse mense laughing at her speaking their language, or about saving up the money for passports, tickets and the rest?

There's a pause as they both stand looking at the village they've known their whole lives, but which soon they will leave behind.

'Can I ask you something, Sara? Is Anton all right, I mean where he is now? Is he happy?' Silence. Sara won't answer his question. He tries again: 'What about Rebekkah?'

More silence.

'Just answer me *this*, then. Will *we* find our happy ending?'

Sara turns to look at him. 'Who is we?'

'Well, me. And Xolani. And you too, I guess. And what about this fokken country?' Hendrik asks the last question for Anton. So that he can know that his brother's sacrifice wasn't for nothing.

Sara sighs. She raises her hand over her eyes, like she's shielding them from the sun while looking into the distance.

'Time will mos tell, hey Hendrik. Time will mos tell.'

Thank you:

Henrietta
Antjie
Graham
Louise
Nadya
Fourie
Sindiwe
Nozolile Zintoyinto
Anisa Zintoyinto
Mamhlote Mazulu
Isak Niehaus
Jolyn Phillips
John Hammer
Herman van der Wilt
Reverend Anthony Henderson and the congregation of
the St Augustus Anglican Church
The Viljoen family

You are the village that helped to make this novel a reality.

The lines of poetry in the epigraph are from Graham
Mort's 'The Work of Water', in *Cusp* (Seren, Bridgend,
2011). Reproduced by permission of the author.